CHARLES WILLIAMS
DEAD CALM

NO EXIT PRESS

1989

No Exit Press
18 Coleswood Road
Harpenden, Herts AL5 1EQ

Copyright © 1963 by Charles Williams

First Published 1963

The right of Charles Williams to be identified as author of this
work has been asserted by him in accordance with the
Copyright, Designs and Patents Act 1988

All rights reserved. No part of this book may be reproduced,
stored in a retrieval system, or transmitted, in any form,
or by any means, electronic, mechanical, photocopying,
recording or otherwise, without the written permission
of the Publishers.

British Library Cataloguing in Publication Data

Williams Charles (1909–1975)
Dead Calm — (No Exit Press)
I. Title
813'.54 (F)

ISBN 0 948353 80 5

9 8 7 6 5 4 3 2 1

Printed and bound in Great Britain by
Cox & Wyman Ltd., Reading

[1]

THOUGH IT HAD BEEN LESS THAN FOUR HOURS SINCE HE'D secured everything on deck and come below, Ingram awoke just at dawn. He turned his head in the faint light inside the cabin and looked at his wife asleep in the opposite bunk. Rae, wearing sleeveless short pajamas of lightweight cotton, was lying on her stomach, her face turned toward him, the mop of tawny hair spread across the pillow encircled by her arms, her legs spread slightly apart and braced, even in sleep, against the motion of the ketch. She never minded, he thought; some people grew irritable and impossible to live with on a sailboat too long becalmed, with its endless rolling and slatting of gear and its annoying and unstoppable noises of objects shifting back and forth in drawers and lockers, but except for an occasional pungent remark when the stove threw something at her she took it uncomplainingly. They weren't in a hurry, she pointed out, they were on their honeymoon, and they had privacy measurable in millions of square miles.

Without even consciously thinking about it, his mind received, filtered, and evaluated each of the individual sounds in the orchestration of creaks and minute collisions going on about him, oblivious to the total melody but capable of becoming instantly alert at the mere suspicion of a note that was out of place. Nothing was rolling or banging on deck; everything was still secure topside. The metallic bumping just beyond his feet in the galley section of the cabin was the teakettle sliding against the rails that kept it on the stove. The click and intermittent rattle above it were dishes shifting minutely inside their stowage on the bulkhead above the sink. The creaking was only a timber working normally as she swung and swung back; if a boat didn't have flexibility it would break up against any kind of sea, like a car smashed against a wall. That sound of something rolling back and forth was a pencil loose in a drawer. The clock struck four bells. He stretched luxuriously. Six a.m. Hot. Dead calm. But at least they'd sailed out of yesterday's grapefruit rinds. They'd had a light southeasterly breeze for six hours last night, which should put them at least another twenty-five miles along their course.

After sliding out of the bunk, he put on water for coffee, moving silently about the galley so as not to disturb Rae. He stripped off his pajamas, picked up a towel, and mounted the companion ladder to the cockpit. Everything on deck was drenched with dew; it stood in great sweaty beads on the brass cover of the binnacle, and the bottoms of the cockpit cushions he'd reversed last night were as wet as if they'd been rained on. It was full daylight now, and the towering escarpments of cloud to the eastward were shot with flame. Not a breath of air stirred; the surface of the Pacific was as unwrinkled as glass except for the heave and surge of the long groundswell running up from the infinite distances of the Southern Hemisphere.

Standing naked in the cockpit, he leaned over and peered into the binnacle from sheer force of habit to check the heading of the ketch as she lay dead in the water except for her rolling. She was lying 290 at the moment, almost abeam to the swell. He turned and looked forward. Everything was secure. Wind or no wind, it was morning, it was beautiful, and it was good to be alive. He was where he wanted to be, at sea with a sound boat and with Rae. They were nineteen days out of the Canal, bound for Tahiti and the islands to the south, tied to no schedule, free of the frustrations and annoyances of life ashore.

He grinned suddenly and made an impatient gesture with his hand. Goofing off. The water for the coffee would be boiling in a few minutes. Reaching inside the companion hatch, he switched off the masthead light, and went forward. Shoved under the lashings of the dinghy atop the deckhouse was a short ladder. He pulled it free, hung it over the port side, stepped over the lifeline, and dived. After coming to the surface, he swam with a powerful crawl stroke up along her side, under the bow, and back down the other side. He turned on his back and floated some fifty feet astern, looking up at her with affection.

Saracen was thirty-two feet on the waterline, forty overall, ketch-rigged. She was mahogany planked over oak frames and had been built less than ten years ago by a New England yard. She wasn't as fast as some, nor as tall and long-ended and patrician of line, but she was reasonably dry on deck and with her short overhang forward and her deep forefoot she pounded very little in a seaway. Deep-water cruising was what she was built for, he thought, and she was good at it. She'd take you there as fast as you needed to go, and she'd bring you back from anything a sane man would take her into.

He swam back, climbed aboard, and stowed the ladder. In the cockpit he rubbed himself down vigorously with the towel and tied it around his middle. He was a big man, no longer young—he was forty-four—with a flat, windburned face and cool gray eyes. The hair was dark, atrociously cut some five days ago by his wife, graying deeply at the temples, and his shoulders and back were hard and rope-muscled, burned dark by the tropical sun. Along his left hip and in back of his left leg were the slick, hairless whorls of old scar tissue, relic of an explosion and fire aboard a boat when he'd operated a shipyard in Puerto Rico, but the limp was long since gone.

He started below to dress and make the coffee, but paused with one foot on the companion ladder to take a last look around the horizon for squalls. They could make up very fast here in the belt of calms along the Line, even in the early morning. There were no clouds that looked suspicious at the moment— His eyes stopped suddenly and returned to the sector off the starboard bow. He'd seen something. Or had he? Yes, there it was again, a tiny speck almost over the rim of the horizon. It disappeared and came into view again. Without removing his eyes from it, he reached inside the hatch and lifted the big seven-by-fifty binoculars from the rack on the after bulkhead. It was a boat.

At that distance, even with the glasses, he could make out nothing about it except that it appeared to be two-masted and was carrying no sail at the moment. He stepped back to the binnacle and checked the heading. It was bearing about 310 degrees. He looked at it again, but it was impossible to tell whether or not anyone was on deck; it was, in fact, visible at all only when it rose to the crest of a swell. Rae would want to see it, he thought; it was the only sign of life they'd sighted since leaving Panama nearly three weeks ago. Well, it'd still be there after breakfast; nobody was going anywhere until they got some wind.

He went below and pulled on khaki shorts and sneakers. The water was boiling now. He measured out the coffee and poured it. While it was running through he wound the chronometer. He checked the barometer, giving it a little tap with his fingernail. It was steady at 29:91. He entered it in the log, along with the time, and the notation, "Calm. PC to clr. Mod. S'ly swell."

Rae rolled over and sat up, yawning. She brushed the tawny mane of hair back from her face and grinned. "Hi, Skipper."

He perched on the side of the bunk and kissed her. "Hi, beautiful."

She made a deprecating gesture. "Everybody's beautiful when he first wakes up. It's called the blotched, rumpled, and bleary-eyed look; beauty shops can't duplicate it. Mmmmm, I was having a wonderful dream."

"About what?" he asked.

"Fresh water. There was a sunken tub about the size of Rhode Island, with two hundred pounds of bath salts in it—"

"Miss all that too much?"

She rumpled his still-wet hair. "Silly. Who'd want to be a clean widow when she could be a dirty sailor's wife?"

"Watch your language, Mate. I just bathed in the Pacific Ocean."

"God, the English language, at seven o'clock in the morning. I mean the dirty wife of a clean sailor."

"Okay, Moonbeam McSwine. How about a cup of coffee?"

"Love it." She swung long bare legs off the bunk and

disappeared into the head, which opened off the narrow passageway between the forward and after compartments. She came out a few minutes later, face washed and hair combed, and sat down on the bunk with her legs braced against the one opposite. He handed her the mug of coffee and a lighted cigarette. "We've got company."

"You mean somebody else is using our ocean?"

He nodded. "I just sighted him."

"Who? Where?"

"Three or four miles away, to the northwest. Looks like a yacht. Yawl or ketch."

"Where do you suppose he's going?"

He grinned. "Nowhere at the moment. He's becalmed too."

"If we could get together and all whistle for wind at the same time, like a grievance committee, or a delegation——"

"This won't last much longer. We whittled off another twenty or thirty miles last night. In a few more days we ought to be picking up the Trades."

"Oh, I'm not complaining. Being becalmed has its points."

"It does?" he asked. "I can only think of one."

"That's the one. Nobody has to be at the wheel."

"I thought you liked to steer."

"I do." She smiled roguishly. "And no further comment, not at this hour of the morning."

"You're a hard woman. Look, I intended to run the engine a few minutes today to dry it out; if you want to, after breakfast we could run over and hail our neighbor. You like to gossip awhile, or borrow a cup of sugar?"

"Sure. But could I have a swim first? Or is he within binocular range?"

"Not unless he's got the Mount Palomar telescope. Anyway, you could wear a suit."

She sniffed. "Swim suit? Fine pagan you are."

After they'd cooked and eaten breakfast and washed the dishes, he returned to the cockpit. The sun was up now, glaring brassily on the polished surface of the sea. *Saracen* had swung around on the swell, but he checked the bearing on the compass and located the other boat without difficulty, using the binoculars. It was off the starboard quarter. Rae came up, wrapped in a terrycloth robe and carrying a towel. "Which way is he?"

He handed her the binoculars and pointed. She searched for a moment. "Mmmmm. There he is. Is he really that small or just so far away?"

"He's a long way off."

She grinned. "Far enough, I think. I can't even tell if there's anybody on deck."

She went forward, hung the ladder over the side, unbelted the robe, and let it drop. She stepped across the lifeline, poised for a moment, dived cleanly, and came to the surface almost immediately with a flip of her head to clear the hair from her eyes. He walked forward along the port side, watching the water around and below her, faintly uneasy as he always was when she was down there. Motion pictures to the contrary, sharks didn't always travel on the surface with their dorsal fins conveniently showing. "Don't go too far from the ladder," he warned.

"I won't."

She swam back and forth several times and came back to the ladder. When she had her feet on the bottom rung and the lifeline in her hands, he said, "Wait there a minute." He turned and ran below, grabbed a saucepan, and pumped a quart of fresh water into it at the sink. She watched, puzzled, as he came hurrying back. He knelt and poured it slowly over her head, washing the salt water out of her hair. She began to laugh, and when he put down the saucepan she sprang the rest of the way up the ladder and threw her arms about him. "It's because I love you," he said, as wet now as she was.

She kissed him again, and then broke up into laughter once more with her face against his throat. "I was thinking of that woman the Taj Mahal was built for."

"Why?"

"When she was alive, I bet even *her* husband didn't pour a whole quart of fresh water in her hair."

"Probably nothing but emeralds."

"The clod." She pushed back. "But I'd better get some

clothes on. They just might have bigger binoculars over there."

He went back to the cockpit. She dried herself with the towel, wrapped it about her head, put on the robe, and went below. The engine controls were in the cockpit. He set the choke, switched on the ignition, and turned it over with the starter. It caught on the third or fourth try, coughed once, and settled down to a steady rumble. He let it idle a few minutes to warm up, and shoved the lever ahead. Taking the wheel, he brought her around and steadied up on the approximate bearing of the other craft. Now that they were under way, the rolling lessened almost miraculously, and the slight breeze of their passage felt cool against his face. He reached for the glasses, picked up the boat again, brought *Saracen* a few degrees to the right to line it up dead ahead, and checked the compass course. Three-fifteen was about right.

"Honey," he called down the hatch, "when you come up, will you bring me a cigar?"

"Right, Skipper. But don't get there too fast. If we're going calling, I've got to dress and put on my face."

"Take your time. It'll take a half-hour or more."

She came on deck in about five minutes, dressed in Bermuda shorts and a white blouse. Her still-damp hair was combed back and tied with a scrap of ribbon, and she'd put on lipstick. He lit the cigar she handed him. She picked up the binoculars and turned forward, searching for the other craft. The sun struck coppery highlights in her hair as she swayed with the motion of the ketch, balancing easily on bare feet.

"Still can't tell whether there's anybody on deck," she said.

"She's a long way off yet," Ingram replied. "And they could be asleep—" He broke off at a muttered exclamation from Rae. "What is it?"

She spoke without lowering the glasses. "I thought I saw something else. Between here and there."

"What?"

"I don't know. It was just a speck, and it's gone now—no. Wait. There it was again."

"Turtle?" he asked.

"No-o. It'd have to be bigger than that; it's too far away. Here, you take a look."

He slid over and stood up in the cockpit. "It's almost dead ahead," she said. "I only had a couple of quick glimpses of it, but I think it was right in line with the other boat and probably three-quarters of the way over to it."

He put a knee on the starboard cockpit cushion and leaned to the right to get out of line with the masts as he adjusted the glasses. He picked up the other craft and studied it for a moment. Ketch-rigged, he thought, and probably a little larger than *Saracen*. There was no one visible on deck. She was almost abeam to the swell and rolling sluggishly. He lowered the glasses a bit and began to search the slickly heaving surface of the sea that lay between.

"See anything?" Rae asked.

"Not yet." Then he did. It was only a speck in the distance, showing for an instant as it rose to the broad crest of a swell. It dropped from view. He marked the location in reference to the other craft and tried to hold the glasses steady to catch it when it came up again. *Saracen* rolled, and he lost it. "Had it," he said. "Wait—here it is again." It was in view for several seconds this time, and he was able to make out what it was. "Dinghy," he announced.

"Adrift?" she asked.

"No. There's somebody in it."

"Odd place to go for a row."

Ingram frowned, still studying the tiny shell. "I think he's coming this way. Must have sighted us and started to row over."

"That's doing it the hard way," she remarked with a puzzled glance at the back of his head. "Why wouldn't he crank up the auxiliary? He must have one."

"I don't know," Ingram said. "Unless it's out of commission."

In another few minutes the dinghy was within easy view without the glasses, continuing to advance across the slick undulations of the sea as its occupant pulled rapidly at the oars, never pausing or even slowing the beat as he turned his head from time to time to check his course. It would have been long since obvious to him that *Saracen* was under way and headed for him, and Ingram wondered why he didn't merely rest on the oars and wait. Judging from the distance remaining to the other yacht, he'd already rowed well over a mile, apparently at that same racing beat. The occupant was a man, bare-headed, wearing a yellow life-jacket.

He was less than a hundred yards away now. Ingram reached down and cut the engine, and in the sudden silence they could hear the creak and rattle of oarlocks as the dinghy came on, its pace unchecked, across the closing gap. *Saracen* slowed and came to rest, slewing around on the swell, port side toward the approaching boat. The man looked around over his shoulder but did not hail. He was going to hit amidships. Ingram stepped quickly up on deck and knelt at the rail. He caught the bow of the dinghy and tried to fend it off, but a last explosive pull at the oars had given it too much momentum, and it bumped away. It swung around against *Saracen*'s side. The man let go the oars. One of them started to slide overboard, but Ingram grabbed it with his other hand and dropped it into the dinghy. "Okay," he said soothingly. "Just take it easy."

The other paid no attention. His lips moved, but he uttered no sound, his eyes reflecting some furious intensity of concentration that excluded all else. Ingram took a turn around a lifeline stanchion with the dinghy's painter and held down a hand to help him on deck. The man caught his arm between elbow and wrist with a grip that made him wince. The other hand caught the stanchion, and he came up all in one plunging and desperate leap that kicked the dinghy backward against its painter and almost capsized it, clawing his way over the lifeline and catching the handrail along the edge of the deckhouse. The suddenness of it caught Ingram unawares, and when the man crashed into him he fell backward and sat down abruptly on the deckhouse coaming. For some reason his glance fell on the other's hand, the one holding on to the handrail. It appeared to be infected from a small wound or cut across the knuckles, but it was the grip itself that caught his attention. The fingers were locked around the handrail so tightly they were flattened and white beneath the tan.

Hunger? he wondered. No, a starving man wouldn't have had the strength to lunge aboard that way. More probably thirst. "Water," he said quietly to Rae. "Not too much."

But she had anticipated the request and was already going down the ladder. The man inched his way aft, clinging tightly to both the lifeline and the handrail along the deckhouse, as though suspended over some terrifying abyss. Ingram followed closely behind him to catch him if he stumbled. The man made it to the cockpit and sank down on one of the cushions, looked around him at the sea with a shuddering motion of his shoulders, and slumped forward with his face in his hands.

Rae came hurrying up the ladder from below with an aluminum cup partly filled with water. Ingram took it and touched the man lightly on the shoulder. "Here you go," he said. "Just take it slowly, and there'll be more in a minute."

The other looked up, blankly at first, and then with dawning comprehension as though aware of them for the first time, and Ingram was conscious of the thought that the face bore none of the ravages he'd always read of as associated with extreme and prolonged thirst—no cracked and blackened lips or swollen tongue. It was, in spite of the growth of golden beard, a boyish and strikingly handsome face, tanned and slender but not haggard, and unmarked by anything except perhaps exhaustion. The gray eyes were red-rimmed as if the man hadn't slept in a long time. Besides the life-jacket he wore only white sneakers and a pair of faded khaki shorts, and it was obvious he was not only quite young, probably still in his early twenties, but powerfully built and in top physical condition.

"Oh," he said. "Thanks. Thanks a lot." He reached for the water, almost indifferently, drank, and put the cup down beside him on the cockpit seat. Ingram saw with surprise that he hadn't even finished it. He drew a hand across his face and made a shaky attempt at a smile. "Man, am I glad to see you." Then he added abruptly, like a small boy suddenly remembering his manners, "My name's Hughie Warriner."

"John Ingram," Ingram said, holding out his hand. "And my wife, Rae." Warriner started to get up, but Rae shook her head and smiled. "No. Just rest."

"What's the trouble?" Ingram asked.

Warriner gestured wearily toward the other yacht rolling on the groundswell a mile away. "She's going down. She's been sinking for days, and I doubt she'll last through the morning."

"What happened?"

"I don't know," the young man replied. "She just seemed to open up all over. I've been at the pump for a week, and almost continuously for the past two days, but I couldn't keep up with it. And since around midnight it's been gaining faster all the time."

Ingram nodded. It would, as she settled lower in the water and additional seams were submerged. Warriner went on, "I thought I was done for, till I looked over here awhile ago and saw you, and then I was scared to death a breeze would come up and you'd go on without ever seeing me. I fired off a couple of flares, but nothing happened. I guess you couldn't see 'em that far away in sunlight—"

"It was probably while we were below eating breakfast, anyway," Ingram said. "And the water's up in your engine now?"

"Yes. But it hasn't worked for a long time anyway. I tried calling you on the radio, but of course if you hadn't seen me you wouldn't have yours turned on, not out here. So my only chance was to try to get over to you with the dinghy before you caught a breeze." He sighed and brushed a hand across his face again. "And am I glad you saw me."

"Yeah, that's cutting it a little fine." Ingram grinned briefly and reached for the ignition key to start the engine again. "But we'd better get on over there. How many aboard?"

"Nobody," Warriner said. "I'm alone."

"Alone?" Involuntarily, Ingram straightened and

looked out across the metallic expanse of sea toward the other yacht. Even at that distance it was obvious she was larger than *Saracen*. "You were trying to take her across the Pacific single-handed?"

"No. There were four of us when we left Santa Barbara . . ." Warriner's voice trailed off, and he stared down at his hands. Then he went on quietly. "My wife and the other couple died ten days ago."

[2]

"OH, HOW AWFUL!" RAE CRIED OUT AND CHECKED HERSELF barely in time to keep from adding, "You poor boy!"—in spite of Warriner's being in the neighborhood of six feet and probably not more than six or eight years younger than she was. Already drawn by the clean-cut, boyish appearance, good looks, and obvious good manners in the face of disaster, she felt a stab of almost motherly compassion and an illogical desire to take him in her arms and comfort him. "How did it happen?" Then she went on hurriedly, "But never mind. You can talk later. Can I get you something to eat? Or some more water?"

"No, thank you, Mrs. Ingram, I'm all right," Warriner replied. "But I could use a cigarette if you have one."

"Of course." She produced them from the pocket of her shorts and held out the lighter. "And why don't you take off that life-jacket? It's hot enough without wearing that thing."

"Oh . . . sure." Warriner looked down at it uncertainly and began unfastening it. He placed it on the seat beside him. "I guess I forgot I had it on."

Ingram's cigar had gone out. He relighted it and tossed the match overboard. "What happened?" he asked.

"It was some kind of food poisoning." Warriner stared somberly at the smoke curling upward from the cigarette forgotten between his fingers. "They all died in one afternoon, within four hours. It was horrible. . . ." He shook his head and then went on in the same flat, mechanical tone. "No, there's no word for what it was like, alone in the middle of the ocean with three people sick and dying, one after the other, all in different stages of the same symptoms, and not being able to do anything about it. And knowing after the first one died there was no hope for the others. My wife was the last one, just at sunset. And the terrible part of it was I wasn't even sick. I just stood there and watched them die, like something that was happening on the other side of a glass wall I couldn't get through."

Rae reached down and put her hand on his shoulder. "I'm sorry," she said. "But don't talk about it now. You've got to get some sleep."

"Thank you," Warriner replied, "but I'm all right. After the first couple of days I managed to snap out of it and get going again. And it was about then I began to notice the bilges were filling up with water and that it took longer every day to pump them out. Before long it was so bad I didn't have time to think about anything but staying afloat. Maybe that was what saved me from cracking up."

"Do you know what the poison was?" Ingram asked.

Warriner nodded. "The only thing it could have been was a can of salmon that must have spoiled. I didn't eat any, because I don't like salmon."

"Had it been opened a long time?"

"No, just a few minutes before they ate it. But it wasn't commercially canned; it was some Russ and Estelle—they were the other couple—some they put up themselves. Every year Russ goes up to the Columbia River for a week's fishing when the Chinook run is on, and when he catches any they have some of it smoked and Estelle cans the rest because Russ claims—I mean, claimed—" Warriner took a deep breath and went on—"claimed it was better than the commercial pack. When we started out on this cruise to Papeete, they had four or five cans left over from last year, so he put them in the stores. About ten days ago—at least, I think it was ten days, I've lost all track of time—it was Estelle's turn to fix dinner. It was hot and muggy and nobody was very hungry. But she happened to remember the salmon and thought she might be able to make some kind of salad out of it by cutting up pickles and onions and putting mayonnaise on it. I didn't eat any; I always figured salmon was for cats, so I made myself a sandwich out of something."

"And nobody noticed anything wrong with it?" Ingram didn't know why he asked. There didn't seem to be much you could do to change the outcome of a tragedy that had happened ten days ago. "The can wasn't bulged or anything?"

"If it was, she didn't notice it. Frankly, she'd had about three rum sours before she went below to fix it. We'd all had, for that matter. And if there was an odor, the onions must have covered it up.

"That was around seven p.m. The next morning between six and six-thirty Russ came up from below—I was at the wheel—and said Estelle was feeling nauseated and upset and wanted to know if I had any idea where those pills were that we'd brought along for the tourist trots. I turned the wheel over to him and went below to look for them.

"I thought they might be in the medicine closet in the head amidships, but when I got down there Estelle was in it, and I could hear her vomiting. When she came out her face was white and sweaty and she looked bad. She didn't have much on, and when she saw it was me instead of Russ she motioned for me to look the other way and ran forward into their cabin. I found the pills and got a glass of water and called out to her. She said it was all right to come in, she was in the bunk. I gave her one. She swallowed it, but she kept rubbing her hand across her face and shaking her head. 'Brother, that rum,' she said. 'It must have had a delayed-action fuse on it.' Her voice sounded funny, as if she had something stuck in her throat.

"I asked her if she was sure it was the rum, and she said, 'I don't know. But you look fuzzy around the edges; I can't get you into focus.' She held out her hand and looked at it and said, 'God, a Picasso hand. It's got seven fingers on it—' "

"What?" Ingram interrupted. He frowned. "Wait a minute—double vision. There's something I've read, or heard—"

"Botulism," Rae said.

"What's that?" Warriner asked. "You mean you don't think it was the salmon?"

"Yes, it probably was the salmon," Rae explained. "Botulism's a very dangerous type of food poisoning that attacks the nervous system. I remember reading an article about it somewhere. I don't remember the other symptoms, but I do recall the double vision and the trouble in speaking or swallowing."

"Do you know what the treatment is?" Warriner asked. "We had a pretty good medicine chest and I tried everything I could think of, but if it turns out that some simple thing we had aboard could have saved them . . ."

Rae shook her head. "You can put your mind at rest about that. I don't think there is any treatment except an antitoxin, which nobody'd have in a first-aid kit. Even if you'd been an M.D. you couldn't have done anything for them."

"Oh. I guess that helps. A little, anyway." Warriner went on. "She looked bad, as I said, but I didn't realize then how sick she was. I guess she didn't either. Anyway, about that time we took two or three heavy rolls and I heard the sails begin to slat, so I went back on deck. I thought the wind had died out again and we'd have to sheet everything in—we'd been becalmed off and on for the past two days, just a capful of breeze now and then from all around the compass. But when I got up in the cockpit, that wasn't it; Russ had left the wheel. He was hanging over the rail, vomiting, and she'd come up into the wind.

"He said he thought he'd got a touch of it too. Even then it'd never occurred to any of us it could be serious; it was just a joke, like the *turista*. I told him where the pills were, and to go back and turn in and not to relieve me at eight unless he was sure he was all over it. He went below.

The breeze held on, fairly steady out of the west; we were making at least four knots, and not too far off the course we wanted, so I didn't want to leave the wheel, even when it was eight o'clock and he didn't come up.

"About eight-thirty I heard somebody moving around in the galley and decided at least one of them was feeling better, but it was Lillian—my wife. She brought me a cup of coffee, and one for herself, and was sitting in the cockpit drinking it when all of a sudden she doubled over with a cramp in her stomach. She ran below to the head. Nobody was able to take the wheel, and *Orpheus* was always a cranky boat; she wouldn't steer herself on any point of sailing. So I doused everything and went below to see how they were. Russ and Estelle were still in their bunks, when they weren't trying to get back and forth to the head. And now *Russ* was complaining that everything looked fuzzy, and he was having trouble talking. Lillian didn't have any symptoms like that yet; she was just nauseated and crampy. But I was beginning to be scared, real scared, thinking of all that empty ocean between us and a doctor. It almost had to be some kind of food poisoning, and everybody decided it must have been the salmon because I hadn't eaten any and I wasn't sick—at least, I wasn't so far. I got the medicine kit out and started through the first-aid handbook that came with it. It was no help; there wasn't anything about food poisoning in it at all, just a lot of jazz about what to do if somebody swallows lye or iodine or something, and how to treat burns and fainting spells and broken bones.

"By ten o'clock Lillian was beginning to have the same symptoms, the fuzzy vision and difficulty in swallowing or talking. The breeze had died out, and it was like an oven below deck with the sun beating down. Russ and Estelle were having trouble breathing. I gave up pawing through the medicines long enough to rig an awning over the cockpit, intending to move them up there, but by now they were too sick to make it up the ladder. I couldn't carry them, not with the boat rolling the way she was, lying becalmed. I rigged wind-chutes, which was stupid, because there wasn't a breath of air moving, but by this time I was so panicky I didn't know what I was doing. I gave them the *turista* pills, and aspirin, and paregoric, and I don't remember what else, but by noon neither Russ nor Estelle could swallow anything any more. They couldn't even talk. All they could do was lie there and fight for breath.

"Russ died a little after three in the afternoon. I hadn't thought there could be anything more horrible in the world than standing there listening to the two of them fighting for breath in that stifling cabin and not being able to do anything to help them, but there was. It was when I realized that only one of them was making that noise now; Russ had stopped. Which meant there was no hope for the others either. Estelle was unconscious by that time, so she didn't know he was dead. Lillian was still conscious and just beginning to fight for breath, but she was in our cabin, aft of the doghouse, so she didn't know either.

"Then Estelle died, less than an hour after Russ. The rest of the day is kind of mixed up and run together; I can only remember crazy pieces of it—Lillian asking me how the others were, and I'd say I'd go see, and I'd go into the forward cabin where they were both dead and then come back and say they were getting much better now and that she'd be over the worst of it in a little while. Then I'd go out of the cabin to pray, so she wouldn't see me. I remember going up on deck once; maybe it would work better up there in the open. I hadn't prayed for anything since I was a kid, and I guess I didn't know how; it struck me once that it seemed like I was trying to negotiate with God, or strike a bargain, or something. I kept saying two of them were gone, couldn't He leave one?

"Lillian died a little after six. When the sound of her breathing stopped, the silence was like something screaming in my ears, and I let go of her and ran up on deck and the sun was just going down. The sky was red in the west, and the sea was like blood, and everywhere there was that terrible silence that went on and on and on as if it was pressing in on me from all around the horizon. . . ." Warriner dropped his face in his hands.

Tears were overflowing Rae's eyes. "I'm sorry," Ingram said, conscious at the same time of something that disturbed him. It was the word *theatrical* intruding on the perimeter of his mind, and he was angry with himself at this apparent callousness. Try it on your own stiff upper lip, he thought, before you throw any rocks; try ten days of it without hearing another voice and you might get a little purple about it too. He wished uncomfortably that he could think of something to add to the simple "I'm sorry," but nothing was going to help the boy except the passage of time. He reached toward the ignition key to start the engine. "But we'd better shag over there and see if we can salvage some of your gear before she goes under."

Warriner shook his head. "There's nothing worth going after. It's all ruined by the water—radio, sextant, chronometer, everything—"

"How about clothes?"

"These will do. Anyway, I don't think I *could* go back aboard. You understand, don't you? It isn't only their dying. Remember, they all died *below deck*. Can you imagine what it was like, what I had to do?"

Ingram nodded.

Warriner's face twisted. "Talk about the dignity of death, and last respects to the dead—pallbearers and bronze caskets and music and flowers. I dragged my wife's body up a companion ladder with a rope—"

"Stop it!" Rae cried out. "You've got to quit thinking about it!"

"I understand," Ingram said. "But you don't have to go aboard; I'll take care of it, if you'll just tell me where to find things—"

"But there's not anything, I tell you!"

"We ought to get your passport," Ingram pointed out. "And whatever money you have aboard. We're bound for Papeete, and you'll need it for your passage home from there. Also, there's a log and ship's papers—"

Warriner gestured impatiently. "The log and ship's papers and passport and money are all pulp and sloshing around in the bilges in three feet of water. If I haven't already pumped them overboard."

"I see," Ingram said, wondering if he did. "But there's another thing. Is she insured?"

"John." Something in Rae's voice made him turn. She went on sweetly, but with a glint in her eyes he'd never seen before. "I don't think we're being very hospitable, or very considerate. Mr. Warriner needs sleep more than anything at the moment, so I'm going to fix a bunk for him. If you'll just come with me and move those sailbags, dear."

She went down the ladder. Ingram followed, conscious of the rigidity of her back as she traversed the rolling cabin and went through the passage at the forward end. The narrow compartment in the eyes of the boat held two bunks, slanted inward toward each other like the sides of a V, but was used only as a locker now. There were cases of food, unopened buckets of paint and varnish, and coils of line, all neatly stowed, and the bunks themselves were piled with bags of sails. There was no hatch above, only a ventilator, and the compartment was dimly lighted by the two small portholes above the bunks.

She pulled the door shut and came close to him. "John Ingram!" It was a whisper, but forceful. "I'm ashamed of you; I never realized you could be this insensitive. Can't you see that boy's on the ragged edge of a nervous breakdown? For heaven's sake, stop asking him questions and let's try to get him to sleep."

"Well, sure, honey," he protested. "I realize what he's been through. But we ought to make *some* attempt to salvage what we can—"

"He doesn't want to go back on there. I'd think you could understand that."

"He doesn't have to. I told him I'd go."

"But why? He said there wasn't anything worth trying to save, didn't he?"

"I know. But obviously water wouldn't ruin everything. Clothes, for instance. Also, he contradicts himself."

"What do you mean?"

"The radio, remember? He said it'd been ruined by the water. But he just got through telling us he had called us on it."

She sighed. "Why do men always have to be so literal? Do you think he's some kind of machine? John, dear, he lost his wife and his two friends all in one afternoon, and then spent the next ten days utterly alone on a sinking boat, and he probably hasn't closed his eyes for a week. I'd be doing well to remember my own name, unless I had it written down somewhere."

"All right—" Ingram began.

"Shhhhh! Not so loud."

"Okay. But you'd think he'd at least want to bring off some of *her* things, wouldn't you? And there was another thing I was about to explain to him. If the boat's insured, he's going to have a hell of a time trying to collect, with no logbook and just his unsupported word she was in sinking condition when he left her—in a dead calm, with no weather making up. The underwriters are going to ask for a statement from me, and I can't corroborate it. How can I? I'll just have to tell 'em she was afloat when I saw her. And that I hadn't even been aboard and didn't know how much water she was taking."

"He said she probably wouldn't last through the morning, and we're not going anywhere in this calm, so we'll still be in sight when she goes down. But let him get some sleep!"

"Sure. God knows, he probably needs it." Still vaguely dissatisfied, he tossed the sailbags into the other bunk and threw a lashing on them. He went back to the cockpit. Warriner was slumped on the starboard seat with the binoculars beside him, as though he'd been looking at the other yacht. Sunlight struck golden fire in his hair, which had been crew-cut originally but had grown long over his ears. Handsome kid, Ingram thought, and then wondered if that could be the reason for his—well, not distrust, exactly. That was overstating it. Call it reservation.

"You asked me if she was insured," Warriner said. "I'm sorry to say she's not. We thought the premium was too high for the risk involved. And also, that if she was lost, we probably would be too."

"Is she pretty old?"

"Yes. Over twenty years. I guess we got stung when we bought her."

"You didn't have her surveyed?"

"Well—yes. That is, not by a professional, but a friend of mine who's real savvy about boats."

Ingram nodded but refrained from any comment. Under the circumstances, it was too much like kicking a man when he was down to elaborate on the foolishness of buying a twenty-year-old yacht without a professional survey, especially since this was a little on the self-evident side at the moment. "You don't know what caused her to open up that way? Have any bad weather?"

Warriner shook his head. "Not recently. That is, except for a few squalls, which never lasted very long. It was just age and general unsoundness."

Ingram was struck by a sudden thought. "You say you were bound from California to Papeete—aren't you pretty far east? Seems to me you'd have crossed the Line nearly a thousand miles west of here."

"We were taking it by stages. Down the Mexican coast to La Paz, and then by way of Clipperton Island." Warriner made an attempt at a smile. "Look, I'm sorry I got dumped on you this way. But I can pull my weight, and it *will* shorten the watches. And I'll keep out of your hair as much as possible; it's not much fun having a third party around."

"Forget it," Ingram said, feeling uncomfortable for some reason. It was the first time he'd ever heard of a shipwreck victim apologizing for his existence, and he tried again to put his finger on exactly what there was about this boy that he couldn't quite like. There didn't seem to be any answer. "Hell, we're just happy we came along when we did."

Warriner made no reply. Ingram picked up the glasses, braced himself against the mizzen boom, and searched out the other yacht. She was near enough now to make out details on deck, but he couldn't tell whether she was any lower in the water than she had been. She wasn't down by the head or stern, but there was no doubt she had water in her, and plenty of it, from the drunken way she lurched on the swell, taking too long to come back each time she rolled. She had a short, rather high deckhouse with windows rather than portholes located near amidships, and in silhouette was vaguely reminiscent of a motor-sailer rather than a conventional sailing yacht. Dumpy-looking, he decided, and probably cranky as hell and slow. Big auxiliary, no doubt, lots of greenhouse for cocktail parties, and probably built for somebody who never used the sails except when he ran out of gas. Still, Warriner probably had upwards of $30,000 invested in her, and it was a sad way for a boat to end. "She's still on an even keel," he said, without lowering the glasses. "You sure we couldn't gain on it, by pumping and bailing together—at least enough to start locating the leaks and calking 'em?"

Warriner shook his head. "It's hopeless. It's been pouring in since around midnight. Nearly six inches in seven hours."

Ingram glanced down at him and then returned to his scrutiny of the other boat without comment, still aware of that nagging sense of dissatisfaction. Something about the whole thing disturbed him, but he couldn't put a finger on it. Just what was it? Warriner was certainly in a position to know how much water was coming into her. And when you stopped to take a good look at it, saving her was only a pipe dream. Even if they could pump her out enough to plug a few of the leaks, the kid would never make land in her alone. She was too big for one man to handle, even without the necessity of being at the pump twelve to fifteen hours a day.

[3]

THE SUN WAS HOTTER NOW. HE TURNED, SEARCHING THE horizon for any darkening of the surface of the sea that would indicate the beginnings of a breeze. Rae came up the ladder. "Your bunk's all ready, Mr. Warriner. Try to sleep until this time tomorrow."

Warriner smiled. "Please call me Hughie. And I don't know how to thank you."

"You don't have to. Just get some rest."

"In a little while. For some reason, I don't feel sleepy at all."

She nodded. "You've been wound too tight for too long. But I know how to fix that." She disappeared down the ladder and came back in a minute with a bottle containing a little over an ounce of whisky. She poured it into the cup that was still beside him. "There's just about enough here to do it." He drained it and accepted the cigarette she held out. "By the time you finish that," she said, "you're going to collapse all over. Just try to make it to the bunk when you feel yourself start to go."

"Thank you," Warriner said. "You're very nice."

She tossed the bottle overboard and perched on the edge of the deckhouse to light a cigarette for herself. The bottle landed with a faint splash just off the port quarter, rolled over as a swell passed under it, and started to fill. It righted itself, its neck out of water. Ingram glanced at it indifferently, and then forward, conscious that Warriner's dinghy was bumping as *Saracen* rose and fell. They'd have to cast it adrift; there was no room to stow it on deck, and of course they couldn't tow it. He looked around and was about to mention this when he stopped, arrested by something in the other's face.

Warriner was staring past him with an almost frozen intensity, apparently at something in the water. Ingram turned, but could see nothing except the bottle, which was about to sink. It had rolled onto its side again as another swell upset it, and water was flowing into its mouth. A few bubbles came up, and it went under. Puzzled, Ingram glanced back at Warriner. The other had risen from his seat and leaned forward, clutching the port lifeline with a white-knuckled grip as he stared down at the bottle falling slowly through sun-lighted water as clear as air. Drops of sweat stood out on his forehead, and his mouth was locked shut as though he were stifling, with an effort of will, some anguished outcry welling up inside him. The bottle was six feet down now, ten, fifteen, but still clearly visible as it continued its unhurried slide into the deepening blue and fading light beyond. Warriner's eyes closed, and Ingram sensed the effort he was making to tear himself away from whatever hell he saw in an innocent and commonplace bottle falling into the depths of the sea, but they came open again almost immediately, still full of the same hypnotic compulsion and horror, like those of a bird impaled on the freezing stare of a snake.

Ingram opened his mouth to ask what the matter was, but caught Rae's eyes on him. She shook her head. They both looked seaward and in a moment heard Warriner sit down again. The whole thing hadn't lasted more than a few seconds. Probably doesn't know we even saw it, Ingram reflected. But what was it? Terror? Terror of what? For some reason he was thinking of the way Warriner had come aboard, the trance-like stare, the convulsive lunge onto the deck, and the way his fingers had flattened themselves around the handrail.

"Breeze coming!" Rae called out suddenly. "Anybody for Papeete?"

Off to the south the surface of the sea was beginning to darken under the riffles of an advancing cat's-paw of wind. Ingram sprang on deck and began casting the gaskets off the mainsail. Rae had run forward and was breaking out the jib. Long months of practice had made them a smoothly functioning team, and by the time they could feel the faint movement of air against their faces a cloud of billowing white Orlon was mounting against the sky. Rae came aft to take the wheel. The mainsail filled. *Saracen* began to move, almost imperceptibly at first, and when she had gathered enough way to come about Ingram looked around and nodded. Rae brought the wheel hard over; she came up into the wind, hung for an instant, and fell off on the port tack, toward the southwest and Tahiti.

For a moment he had forgotten Warriner, but when he turned from setting up the mainsheet to trim the jib, he found the other already hauling on it. Warriner threw it on the cleat and straightened. "How about the mizzen?"

Ingram nodded and began taking off the gaskets.

"Might as well get everything on her; the breeze might last for a while. But you go ahead and turn in."

Warriner smiled. "I think I will, as soon as we get this up." He seemed to have recovered completely from the horror of a few minutes ago. They hoisted the mizzen and trimmed the sheet. Ingram leaned over to look in the binnacle. "Can we make 235?" he asked Rae.

"Easy," she replied. "We're to windward of that now." She came right a little. "Here we are—230 . . . 233 . . . 235."

Ingram glanced aloft at the strands of ribbon on the shrouds and started the mainsheet a little. *Saracen* heeled slightly under a puff and began to gather way. He turned to Warriner. "We're going to have to cast your dinghy adrift. No room to stow it."

Warriner nodded. "Yes. Of course."

Ingram loosed the painter from the lifeline stanchion, coiled it, dropped it into the dinghy, and gave the boat a push away from the side. It drifted back and began to fall behind in the wake, riding like a cork over the broad undulations of the swell. Warriner had turned and was staring toward the other yacht, which was off the starboard quarter now that they had come about. The dinghy was a hundred yards astern, growing smaller and looking lost and forlorn in the immensity of the sea.

"Well, if it's all right with you, I guess I'll turn in," he said at last. "If the breeze holds, I can take over tonight."

"Don't worry about it," Rae said. "You'd better rest for a couple of days. There'll be something for you to eat when you wake up."

"It'll be pretty hot down there," Ingram added, "but if you leave the door open you'll get a little circulation of air from the ventilator."

Warriner nodded and went down the ladder. He paused once to turn for a last look at the other boat before his head disappeared below the level of the hatch. When Ingram looked around at Rae, her eyes were misted with tears. He leaned forward and peered down the hatch. Warriner was going through the passage into the forward compartment. He couldn't hear them if they spoke in normal tones.

He slid back close beside her. "What do you make of it?"

"That thing about the bottle?"

"Yes."

She shook her head. "I don't know. But grief does strange things—grief and complete isolation."

"But just a sinking bottle—"

"Obviously it wasn't a bottle he was seeing." She paused, her eyes fixed moodily on the compass card. Then she went on, "What's a sea burial like?"

"I've never seen one, thank God, but from what I've read, you sew the body in canvas and weight it with something. Why?"

"I'm not sure, but . . ." She gestured helplessly.

"I think I know what you mean," Ingram said. "But I'm not sure I agree with you." Wrapped in white Orlon, with the water this clear and the boat lying dead in the water above them, the bodies would still be visible a long way down if you wanted to torture yourself by leaning over the side and watching them disappear into the dark down there. "But that's only morbid. This was worse. Horror—I don't know what you'd call it."

She nodded thoughtfully. "I know. But being utterly alone afterward . . ." Her voice trailed off. The breeze had dropped to a whisper. *Saracen* ghosted through the bald spot for a few yards, the sails beginning to slat; then it picked up again, only to die out once more in less than fifteen minutes. *Saracen* rolled heavily, booms aswing. Ingram sheeted them in. He stood up, still disturbed, and annoyed at himself because he didn't know why, and trained the binoculars on the other yacht. Then, with a gesture of impatience, he made up his mind.

"I'm going aboard her."

Rae looked up. "Why?"

"I don't know. There's something about the whole damned thing I can't quite swallow; no matter how I turn it, it won't go down. Look, Rae, anybody who managed to get this far from land in a boat without killing himself must be a sailor, and that's not the way a sailor abandons one. Just because somebody else comes along going in the same direction—like a hitch-hiker. You'd bring something off, or you'd go back for what you could salvage."

"You don't believe she's sinking?"

"All I know is she's still afloat." He continued to study the other yacht. As far as he could tell, there was no change in her trim or amount of freeboard. Well, it didn't mean anything, actually; it could be hours, or even days, before she went under. He was probably being silly.

"Did he say whether she was insured or not?" she asked.

"He says she's not."

"Then it'd be pretty expensive, wouldn't it, just going off and leaving her in the middle of the ocean?"

He frowned. "Yes, but that's still not what I mean. If she's leaking at all, he'd never make port in her alone; she's too big for singlehanded sailing, to say nothing of being at the pump all the time. He almost has to abandon her, but not the way he did. I keep getting the feeling he doesn't wany *anybody* to go aboard."

"But why?"

"I don't know. Admittedly, it doesn't make any sense. But look—you'll notice he didn't turn in until we were under way. And had cast his dinghy adrift."

"That was probably just coincidence."

"Sure. It could be."

"You're going to put our dinghy over?" Rae asked.

"No." He turned, searching for the other one. He could still see it when it crested a swell, several hundred yards astern. "We'll pick his up again. No strain, if we get another breeze."

Saracen had begun to swing around on the swell, to a southerly and then a southeasterly heading. Ingram stood up again with the glasses and could see the water beginning to darken once more to the southward. He looked at his watch. It had been nearly thirty minutes since Warriner had gone below. He slipped down the ladder, crossed to the passage going into the forward compartment, and looked in. Warriner lay on his back, his eyes closed, breathing heavily.

He came back to the cockpit just as the breeze began to stir again. It was out of the south, to starboard on the heading they were on now, and the other yacht lay perhaps a mile and a half away on the port bow, with the dinghy somewhere in between. *Saracen* began to move ahead. He motioned for Rae to steady up where she was, and stepped forward to search out the dinghy. In a moment he saw it top a swell almost dead ahead. There was a long boathook lashed atop the deckhouse. He slid it free and looked down to windward, hoping the breeze would continue strong enough to give them steerageway. As far as he could see the surface was riffled and dark. He stepped back to the break of the deckhouse and spoke quietly to Rae. "See it?"

She nodded. "Now and then. When it comes up."

"Good. We'll take it on the starboard side."

Five minutes passed. The breeze faltered but came on again before they lost steerageway. It was less than fifty yards away now. Ingram motioned her a little to port and stood ready with the boathook. The dinghy began to slide past along the starboard side, less than ten feet off. He hooked it neatly at the bow, hauled it inward, and got hold of the painter. He led it aft and made it fast with a grin at Rae. "Nice going."

It was a run almost downwind now to the other yacht. He started the main and mizzen sheets and studied her through the glasses. She was lying on a westerly heading, abeam to the breeze. "Right just a little," he said to Rae. "We'll come up astern and lay to about a hundred yards off."

The gap began to close slowly, and then more slowly as the breeze faltered. It stopped altogether, and the sea became like heaving billows of silk, blinding off to starboard with the glare of the sun. Then, just before *Saracen* began to yaw on the swell, it came on again. The sails filled. The distance was less than a half-mile now.

"I don't like that sluggish way she rolls," Rae said.

"She's got water in her, all right," Ingram agreed.

"Are you sure it's safe to go aboard?"

"Sure. She won't capsize, with all that keel under her. And she won't go under all at once."

"But suppose you're below? You might get trapped."

"I won't go below if she's that close. I can tell when I get on her."

They were still over two hundred yards away when the breeze died again. *Saracen* drifted forward a few yards and began to wallow as she slewed around. Ingram surveyed the remaining distance with exasperation, and searched the horizon on all sides. "Slick as a bald head," he said and sheeted the booms in. "This'll have to do. I'm going aboard."

"Why not start the engine?" she asked.

"He might wake up."

"I doubt it." Then she caught his meaning. "Why? What difference does it make if he does?"

He hesitated; then he shrugged. "I don't like the idea of leaving you on here alone with him. Unless he's asleep, I mean."

"Why, for heaven's sake?"

"I don't know. It's stupid, I realize, but there's just something about him I don't quite buy. Not till I know more about him."

"Well, of all the worriers."

He grunted. "You're probably right. But let him sleep, anyway." He loosed the dinghy's painter and hauled the boat up alongside. Before he stepped down into it he took a careful look around the horizon for squalls. It could be highly dangerous if one made up suddenly while Rae was alone, with all sail on her. There was nothing, however, that looked even remotely suspicious. "If you get another whisper of breeze," he said, "work her on down and come about off the stern. I won't be long."

"Right. You will be careful, won't you?"

"Sure."

"Wait. Don't you want to put on that life-jacket?" It was still lying where Warriner had taken it off.

He grinned. "What for?" Nobody could capsize a dinghy in a sea like this. At the same time, he wondered why Warriner had been wearing it. Timing himself with *Saracen*'s roll, he stepped lightly down into the dinghy and pushed away from the side.

It rode like a chip on the oily groundswell, and reflected sunlight glared in his face as he shipped the oars and began pulling toward the other yacht. As he drew nearer, he could see the sails were sloppily furled and that the deck was littered with an unseamanlike mess of uncoiled and unstowed lines. The main boom rested on its gallows frame, but the mizzen swung forlornly back and forth, banging against its slackened sheets. She was at least six inches below her normal waterline, he thought, and her movements were heavy and sluggish, like those of a dying animal, as she lurched over and back under the punishing rays of the sun. He felt sorry for her, as he always did for a boat in trouble. He changed course slightly to pass under her stern and come up on her starboard side. Her name and home port were spelled out in ornate black letters edged with gilt against the white paint of her transom.

ORPHEUS
SANTA BARBARA

He was still some twenty yards away, rounding her stern, when he heard a crash from somewhere inside the hull, followed in a moment by another. Apparently something had come adrift, a drawer or a locker, and was slamming back and forth on the water inside her. He pulled quickly up along the starboard side and, as she rolled down on the swell, caught one of the lifeline stanchions. After shipping the oars, he gathered up the painter and stepped on deck. He was near amidships, opposite the doghouse. As he made the painter fast he could hear the flow and splash of water inside her hull, sweeping from side to side as she rolled. He didn't like the feel of her under his feet. Better make it short, he thought.

Aft of the doghouse was a slightly raised deck, enclosed by a low railing, which extended back almost to the mizzenmast and the helmsman's cockpit. There was a skylight in the center of this, apparently above the after cabin. It was closed and secured. He stepped aft, feeling her unsteady lurch as she rolled, ducked under the main boom, and looked into the doghouse hatch. There were only four steps leading down, since the top of it was quite high above the deck outside. There was no water here, but the deck was covered with a litter of charts and scratch pads and pencils from a drawer that had slid out of the chart table on the starboard side. He came on down the steps and looked quickly around. The port side and that part of the starboard side forward of the chart table were taken up with settees covered with some white plastic material. On racks above the chart table were a radio-telephone and radio direction-finder.

Aft, beside the steps leading up on deck, was a low doorway, and amidships at the forward end was another. The latter was open. He stepped over to it and peered through. Steps led downward to the main cabin, which was in ruin. At the after end, on the port side, were a sink, stove, refrigerator, and stowage cupboards, while to starboard was a table surrounded on two sides by a leather-covered settee. Everything was drowned, and the cabin was filled with the dank odor of wetness and decay. Water at least two feet deep swirled back and forth, crashing into the stove and refrigerator and settee and dripping from the bulkheads and ceiling, all intermingled with rolling cans from some burst locker, sodden articles of clothing, and books from an emptied bookshelf. It was sickening. At the forward end was a doorway which probably opened into a lavatory, and to the left of it a curtained passage to the forward cabin. He stepped down and splashed through the swirling debris to the passage and peered in. The two bunks were rumpled and dripping, and water rocked back and forth between them. It was just as Warriner had said. He wondered what he was looking for.

He turned and hurried back to the doghouse. Through the windows he caught a quick glimpse of *Saracen* gracefully riding the groundswell two hundred yards away, still becalmed. The mere sight of her was comforting after the ruin below. The door at the aft end of the doghouse was closed and secured with a hasp, through the staple of which a pair of dividers had been dropped. He pulled the dividers out, and as he turned to toss them on the chart table his eye fell on the ship's log, behind a clip on the bulkhead above it. He frowned, puzzled. Warriner had apparently been telling the truth otherwise, so why had he lied about that? He'd said the logbook was pulp, sloshing around in the bilges. And that the radio and chronometer and sextant were all ruined. Nothing up here was wet at all. And as water rose in the cabins below, wouldn't he have brought his passport and money and other valuables up here where they'd stay dry? It would be the natural thing to do. They might be in one of the other drawers of the chart table. Well, he'd look for them in a minute. He pushed open the door and peered down into the after cabin.

A dark-haired woman who appeared at first glance to be completely nude was huddled on the far end of the right-hand bunk, her back against the bulkhead at the foot of it and her legs drawn up under her chin as if to get as far as possible from the door. One hand was up to her mouth and her eyes were wide with fear, which changed to amazement and disbelief as she stared into his face. She cried out, "Stop! Stop, it's not him!" And in the same fraction of a second Ingram saw the other one reflected in the panel mirror mounted on the after bulkhead between the bunks. A man was standing just below him, to the left of the steps leading down, a big man, naked from the waist up, with a broad, beard-stubbled face smeared pink with diluted blood running down from a wound somewhere in the sodden mess of his hair. In his upraised hand was a billet of wood, apparently the end of a drawer he'd pulled from under one of the bunks and smashed. He'd been poised to bring it down on Ingram's head, and when the girl's piercing outcry stopped him he tried to recover. At the same moment *Orpheus* lurched over to starboard, and he fell into the water washing back and forth across the cabin sole. He pushed himself to a sitting position in the water with his back against the other bunk, brushed a hand across his bloody face, and looked up at Ingram with a hard and bitter grin.

"Welcome to Happy Valley," he said. "Where's the All-American psycho?"

"Get on deck!" Ingram snapped. "I'll be back." He whirled and plunged up the steps into the open, ducked under the main boom, and dropped into the dinghy. His hands fumbled as he loosed the painter. Two explosive strokes with the oars brought him into the clear past *Orpheus*'s stern, where he could see across to *Saracen*. Her position was unchanged except that she had swung around and was lying broadside to.

Rae was alone in the cockpit.

He breathed softly and dug in the oars, feeling sweat begin to run down into his eyes. He came up the broad slope of a swell and ran down the other side like some frenzied, two-legged waterbeetle in flight for its life. It's all right, he told himself. It's all right. There's no reason the crazy son of a bitch would wake up. Then, across a hundred and fifty yards of open water, he heard the growl of the starter. Rae was coming to pick him up.

[4]

HE TRIED TO SIGNAL TO HER. AT THE RISK OF CAPSIZING, he stood up in the dinghy and frantically sliced the air in horizontal sweeps of his opened hands, but she was bent over the controls now and didn't see. The starter growled again, and this time the engine started with a coughing backfire that spread gooseflesh between his shoulderblades. One of his oars started to slide overboard. He grabbed it and dropped to the seat again. Muscles writhed across his back as he dug them in and lunged, flinging the dinghy up the side of the swell. He was to blame. She'd been watching with the glasses and had seen the way he'd exploded out of the doghouse and run across the deck, and, knowing only that there was something urgent about his getting back, was trying to help. *Saracen* was swinging now, under way and foreshortened as she began to bear down upon him. The gap was only a hundred yards, and closing. Some of the fear began to leave him. It was going to be all right. He heard her cut back the throttle and drop the engine out of gear. Then when he turned his head again he felt himself grow cold all over. There was a spot of golden color just to the left of the lined-up masts. It was Warriner's head. He was standing on the companion ladder, looking aft.

Nothing seemed to move. There was a piercing clarity about every detail of the scene—the foreshortened hull pointed toward him, the little curl of bow wave under her forefoot, the tall spires of Orlon achingly white against the sky, and just this side of Rae's face that spot of gold like a medallion poised on edge above the cambered top of the deckhouse—but the whole thing was frozen like a single frame of motion-picture film with the projector jammed. *Saracen* was seventy-five yards away, with Warriner's head just beginning to turn. A few seconds either way could decide it, but they were something over which he no longer had any control.

Maybe nothing would happen. Maybe he actually *had* forgotten the people he'd locked in there to drown. Or if he'd really been asleep, maybe his reaction time would be off just enough to make the difference— The film jerked then, between the down-thrust oars and the stroke, and the projector began to run. Warriner's head swung on around, and he saw the dinghy and the sinking *Orpheus* beyond. He leaped the rest of the way into the cockpit, and his figure merged with Rae's.

Ingram heard the engine race, still out of gear. It slowed and came back up again almost in the same instant, with the load on it now. Which way would he turn? At the risk of a fraction of a second's raggedness in the beat of the oars, he had to turn his head and look. *Saracen* loomed over him less than four lengths away, the gap closing faster now as she gathered speed, but she was already beginning to swing to starboard. He dug in his left oar and spun the dinghy around almost at right angles to cut across her course.

Saracen, in a hard-over right turn, was on his left now. He could see Rae fighting to reach the ignition switch. Warriner, holding the wheel with one hand, threw her back. She fell to her knees on the short section of deck aft of the cockpit, but sprang up and flung herself on him again. Ingram's eyes stung with sweat, and the oars were bending as he threw the dinghy forward. The engine roared at full throttle; *Saracen's* bow was swinging off faster now than he was gaining, but the stern was still coming down toward him. Twenty yards . . . fifteen . . . The locked and struggling figures in the cockpit suddenly burst apart. Warriner's fist swung, and Ingram saw her fall. She lay in a crumpled heap on the afterdeck, unmoving, one arm dangling over the stern as if she were calling out for help. Ten yards . . . four . . . three . . . The turn was completed now, and the stern was beginning to draw away from him. He gave one more desperate heave on the oars, stood up, and flung himself at the rail. The dinghy kicked backward under him. His outstretched hands were two feet short, and then he was in the churning white water under the quarter.

He was already behind the propeller, or he might have lost an arm. He felt the solid kick of the water thrown back from it whirl him over, and then his head was above surface and *Saracen's* stern was ten yards away. It dipped as her bow rose to an oncoming swell, and for an instant he could see Rae's figure face down on the afterdeck, her hair very dark against the bleached and weathered teak. "Jump!" he yelled. "Jump! Get off!" She lay motionless.

For the first time in his life at sea he completely lost his head. It lasted for only a moment, and when he realized what he was doing, that he was threshing madly at the water, trying to swim after *Saracen's* receding stern, he got control of the panic inside him and brought himself up. Lifting his face above water, he roared out once more with all his remaining breath, "Jump, Rae! Jump!" The limp and dangling arm was his only answer. She was either badly hurt or unconscious.

The dinghy was behind him. Both oars had slipped overboard. He found them, threw them back in, and lifted himself in over the transom. He was more scared than he had ever been in his life, and the whole scene came to him through the winy haze of a desire to get his hands on Warriner and kill him, but there was no time to give way to futile emotion. He whirled the dinghy about and sent it racing across the two hundred yards of open water toward *Orpheus,* trying not even to think except of what he had to do, as if it were an exercise. *Saracen* was going straight away, and he could still see Rae's figure on the stern.

He turned his head. The man and woman had come on deck and were standing just aft of the doghouse, watching him. He shot the dinghy across the few remaining yards, slammed into *Orpheus*'s port side, and pulled in the oars. Neither of them had made a move to take the painter. He grabbed it himself, leaped on deck, and made it fast. "Have you got any glasses?" he asked.

The man grinned bleakly. "You didn't seem to do any better than we did. Maybe you have to be crazy yourself to outguess him."

Ingram caught himself just short of smashing him in the face—not because the man was already hurt or because he was probably in no way to blame, but merely because it would waste time. "Binoculars?" he asked again. "Where are they?"

The man jerked a thumb toward the doghouse. "Rack, just inside the door." But the woman had already taken a step down the ladder and reached for them. Ingram lifted them from her hand without thanks, without even seeing her, and whirled, bringing them to bear on *Saracen*. She was still going straight away on the same course. As he adjusted the knob, she leaped sharply into focus, every detail distinct. Rae still lay huddled on the afterdeck, as far as he could tell in the same position. Warriner was at the wheel, looking forward, apparently into the binnacle. Maybe he had forgotten she was there. Then Ingram realized the futility of any conjecture as to what went on in Warriner's mind. "Have you got a spare compass?" he asked without lowering the binoculars. "Boat compass, or a telltale in one of the cabins—"

"There's a little one in a box in the chartroom," the man said.

"Get it," Ingram ordered, "and set it in the dinghy. Then put your azimuth ring on the steering compass and keep calling out the bearing of that boat."

"And what's all that jazz for?" the man asked. He hadn't moved.

Ingram lowered the glasses then and looked at him for the first time. "You do what I tell you to, you son of a bitch," he said, "and do it now. My wife's still on there. If he throws her overboard, I want to know where. And if I don't get to her in time because I didn't have a course, and a compass in that dinghy, you'll go next."

"Just a minute, friend—" the man began, but Ingram had already turned away and locked the glasses on *Saracen* again. She was at least a half-mile away; he could still see Rae lying on deck, but less clearly now. He heard the woman say, "Oh, stop it; just do as he says. You find the compass, and I'll get the azimuth ring." He paid no attention. He was trying to make a cold appraisal of the several possibilities while at the same time struggling in the back of his mind with the dark animal of fear. This might be the last time he would ever see her, this dwindling spot of color fading away toward the outer limit of binoculars, but that was something he couldn't think about. If he lost his head, there was no chance at all.

She must be still unconscious, because as far as he could tell she hadn't moved. If Warriner threw her over now, while she was still out, she'd drown. The longer he waited, the more chance there was she'd be conscious and able to swim, but on the other hand, the farther out she was, the more it increased the odds against finding her in time, even with a compass course to follow. In a dinghy you were too low in the water, with a groundswell that was running higher than your head. And he *had* to see when it happened.

It was already growing difficult to make out the deck. He was too low. He tore his eyes away from the glasses long enough to leap up on the doghouse and brace his legs against the doomed and melancholy rolling of the boat, and for an instant he was conscious again of the forlorn banging of her gear and the rushing sound of water inside the hull. If he got her back, they'd only drown together when this derelict finally gave up and died. Well, you could only take one thing at a time.

Somebody was calling him from the cockpit. It was the woman. "Bearing 240 degrees."

"Thanks," he said, without looking around. It was difficult to hold the glasses steady enough now to make out the figures on deck; Warriner must be still running the engine at nearly full throttle, to be that far away. Rae was still there, but in another few minutes he wouldn't be able to see her at all. But if Warriner let go the wheel long enough to put her over, *Saracen* would swing around; that he'd be able to see.

"No change. Still 240," the woman said.

"Right."

Minutes dragged by. He lost all track of time. His arms ached, trying to hold the glasses still. The sun beat down on his head, and he could feel sweat run in little rivulets across his face. He could no longer see *Saracen*'s deck at all, but her course continued straight on toward the southwest without a bobble. She must be still there. . . .

"Still 240."

It was hopeless now; he might as well admit it. Even if he knew exactly where it happened, the odds were astronomical against finding her in time at that distance. It would take the dinghy three-quarters of an hour to get there, and even the slightest deviation from the course would increase the area by square miles of rolling ocean, all of it exactly alike.

"That'll do for the moment," he called out to the woman. "Your auxiliary's under water? I mean, it won't run at all?"

"No," she said. "It's completely submerged. There's no fuel, anyway; we used it all."

He swung the glasses, searching for signs of wind. It would take a half-gale, he thought, to move this cistern through the water, even if they could keep it afloat. As far as he could see in every direction, the surface was as slick as oil. *Saracen* was hull down, fading over the rim of the horizon. Swept by fear for Rae and black rage at his own helplessness, he wanted to curse and slam the binoculars through the doghouse roof. Instead, he leaped down on deck and turned to the man, who was in the cockpit beside the woman. "How long have you been pumping?"

"It's been getting a little worse every day for the past two weeks," the other replied.

"And you haven't been able to hold it at all, or locate the leaks?"

"I think all her seams are opening up. We could keep up with it at first by pumping two or three hours a day. After a while it took six. And for the past thirty-six hours there's been somebody on the pump every minute—that is, till around sunup this morning, when he slugged me and locked us in there. No warning at all—the crazy bastard just blew his gasket and tried to kill us—"

Ingram cut him off. "We haven't got time for the story of your life. How bad's that cut on your head?"

The other shrugged. "I'll live. Long enough to drown, anyway."

"Better have it looked after." Ingram addressed the woman. "Take him below and clean it and put Mercurochrome or something on it. If it needs stitches, cut the hair away, and call me—I mean, if you've got sutures and a needle. When you come back, bring up two buckets and a couple of pieces of line eight or ten feet long."

"What for?" the man asked.

Ingram turned toward him. "That's twice you've asked me that when I told you to do something. Don't do it again."

The other's grin hardened. "So don't throw your weight so hard, sport; you might throw it overboard. You may be Captain Bligh on your own boat—"

Ingram walked back to the break of the raised deck and stood looking down at him. "You finished?"

"For the moment. Why?"

"I'm going to tell you, if you're sure you've said all

you've got to say. You mentioned my boat." He gestured bleakly toward the southwest. "There it goes. My wife's on it, with a maniac, unless he's already killed her. I don't know what he is to you, and I don't care, but he came off this boat, if you follow me. So let's understand each other, once and for all; we're going after him in this tub if we have to walk and carry it on our backs, and it's going to stay afloat if you have to drink the water out of it with a straw. I haven't got time to kiss you or draw you a diagram every time I tell you to do something, so don't ask me any questions. And I'm pretty close to the edge, so don't bump me. That clear now?"

There was no fear in the other's eyes and no bluster, only that hard-bitten humor. "Sounds fair enough, sport, if you know what you're doing. But be sure you do; I'm allergic to stupid orders."

"Right," Ingram said. "How about the radio?"

"Kaput."

"The receiver too?"

"Yeah. Whole thing was powered by the main batteries."

"Why didn't you bring the batteries up here somewhere before the water covered them? That occur to you?"

"They were already discharged. No more gas for the generator."

No power, no radio, no lights, Ingram thought bitterly. "All right. Go fix your head. And don't be gone all day."

They went below. He turned to the pump, which was located against the after side of the doghouse. It had a stirrup handle which was normally covered by a plate flush with the surface of the deck when stowed, but the plate was off now, the handle extending upward. Warriner was up here alone, pumping, when he sighted us, he thought. But instead of calling the others, he slugged the man and locked them in the cabin. Why? He muttered savagely and grabbed the handle; there was no time to waste wondering about the motivations of a psychopath. It was a good pump that could lift a lot of water, and there was no indication of its being clogged. He could hear the water going overboard in a solid-sounding stream as his back bent and straightened.

He started to think of Rae and then tried furiously to make his mind go blank. He'd go crazy. He stepped up the tempo of his pumping. Where the hell were those two? Were they going to take the rest of the summer? Then he realized they hadn't been gone five minutes. They came back up, carrying two ten-quart buckets, one of them apparently the gurry-bucket from the galley. The man was carrying a length of small line. The blood was washed from his face, and he was wearing a Mexican straw hat with an untrimmed and unbound brim, to protect his head from the sun. "No hemstitching necessary," he said.

"Okay. Take the pump a minute," Ingram directed.

"Jawohl, mein Führer." He grabbed the handle as Ingram let go, and began throwing a hard, steady stream of water over the side. Ingram glanced at him as he stepped back to the cockpit. Clown? Hard case? Idiot? What difference did it make? The azimuth ring was still on the campass. When *Orpheus* rose to a swell he got a snap bearing of the tiny feathertip of white that was all that remained now of *Saracen's* mainsail. It was 242 degrees. Apparently Warriner was still holding the same course. What did that mean? Anything, or nothing, he thought. Dealing with a deranged mind—what was the use even trying to guess?

The ventilating hatch above the after cabin was closed and secured with a steel pin. He slid the pin out and threw the cover all the way back on deck. The opening was on the centerline, directly above the space between the two bunks below. The other two watched, the man continuing to pump, while he grabbed up the line, cut off a piece about eight feet long, and made one end fast to one of the buckets. He dropped it through the opening, gave a flip of the line to upend it as it landed in the water swirling back and forth across the cabin sole, and hauled it up again hand over hand. He pivoted and threw the water over the side. It was going to work, but it was awkward because of the main boom, which was directly over the opening. He freed the end of it from its notch in the center of the gallows frame, shoved it out to the end, and lashed it. It was all right now. He could stand right over the hatch with his legs on opposite sides. He dropped the bucket again, filled it, and flung the water overboard.

"Okay, let your wife take the pump," he said to the man. "That's a little easier. You bail here."

The man made a burlesque bow to the woman, with a flourish toward the pump. "Pamela, little helpmeet—'

"Shut up," she said. She began pumping. There was something puzzling about the exchange. Ingram didn't know what it was—or care.

He handed the man the bucket. "You know how to dip water at the end of a line?'

"Well, I once poured some out of a boot. Not that I like to brag—"

"Have at it," Ingram said.

The bucket landed on its side, shipped a pint of water, came upright, and floated. After yanking the line back and forth a half-dozen times, the man succeeded finally in sinking it. He hauled the water up.

"I meant without taking all day," Ingram said. "Look." He demonstrated, flipping the bucket so it landed in a dipping position and came up full all in one motion. "I want five or six buckets a minute out of there."

"Think it'll do any good?"

"I don't know," Ingram replied curtly. "But you haven't been able to keep up with it with the pump alone. If we don't gain on it this way, put on your swim trunks. The nearest land's over that way, twelve hundred miles."

"Geez, don't scare me like that. For a minute I thought you said twelve thousand."

Ingram turned away without reply and gathered up the other bucket and the rest of the line. Between the forward side of the doghouse and the foot of the mainmast was another hatch, secured with dogs. He kicked the dogs loose with his feet and opened it. It was over the centerline of the main cabin, and in the dim light below he could see the debris-laden water pouring mournfully back and forth as *Orpheus* rolled. He made the line fast to the bucket and dropped it. He hauled it up, full, and threw the water overboard. This near the mainmast, the boom was in his way, and he had to crouch to avoid it. It was uncomfortable, and after a while it would be back-breaking.

Drop . . . haul . . . turn . . . throw . . . He counted. It was nine seconds. Call it a conservative six buckets a minute—ten a minute between them. They were ten-quart buckets, twenty pounds of water. Six tons of water an hour, with maybe half that much more from the pump. They'd soon know how fast it was coming in; if they didn't lower it this way, and damned fast, they were done for. They couldn't keep up this pace for very long, all three of them working at once. Somebody had to sleep, and if they ever got a breeze one had to be at the wheel.

There was something else that had to be done, too, within the next few minutes. He straightened, looking down toward the southwest. There was no trace now of *Saracen*; she was gone over the horizon. He reached up and unshackled the halyard from the head of the mainsail and made a sling from what was left of the line they'd brought up, leaving a free end about four feet long. He shackled the sling to the end of the halyard, retrieved the binoculars, and slung them about his neck.

"I'll need both of you for a few minutes," he called out to the man. They came forward. "Think you can hoist me to the top of the mast?"

"Sure." The other looked up at the spar swinging its dizzy arc across the sky. "Better you than me."

"Why not me?" the woman said. "I'm the lightest."

Ingram shook his head. "It's not easy. If you lost the mast it'd beat you to jelly before we could get you down."

He didn't like the prospect himself, with *Orpheus* rolling her rails under and two people he didn't know on the other end of the line, but there was no help for it. He loosed the halyard fall from the pin on the forward side of the mast. "Keep a turn around the pin," he said. "And take it slow. When I get up to the spreaders I'll tell you when to stop and when to heave."

He climbed atop the boom, stepped into the sling, took a turn around the mast with the free end of the line, and made it fast to the shackle. "Okay. Hoist away." The halyard came taut, with his weight suspended in the sling, and he began to move upward in short jerks, two or three feet at a time, with his legs locked around it while he pulled upward with his arms. The first twenty feet were not too bad, but as he continued to mount his arc increased, both in distance and in velocity, with the resultant snap at the end more abrupt and punishing. He reached the spreaders, the horizontal members extending out at right angles to the mast. This was the dangerous part. He had to cast off his safety belt momentarily in order to pass it around the mast above them.

"Hold it a minute," he called out. With both legs and one arm locked around the mast, he worked at the knot with his free hand. It came loose. If he lost his grip now he'd swing out and then back against the mast with enough force to break his skull. The mast swung down to starboard, snapped abruptly at the end, and came back. His arms and legs were slick with sweat, almost frictionless against the varnished surface. He changed arms, caught the dangling piece of line with his right hand, passed it up over the spreader and around the mast. Gripping the mast with his right arm again, he made the end of the line fast once more to the shackle with his left hand, working solely by feel.

"Up easy," he called out. "Slow. About two feet."

He came up, got one leg across the spreader, and then the other. "Okay, hoist away." He went on up. Three feet from the masthead light and the blocks at the top of the mast, he called out, "That'll do. Make it fast." He hoped they knew how.

This was no place for a queasy stomach, he thought. It was like riding a bucking horse making forty feet at a bound. While he was groping for the binoculars he looked down at the deck sixty feet below. Most of the time he was out over the water; he crossed the deck only through the vertical sector of his swing from one side to the other. The centrifugal force at the end of the roll when the mast stopped abruptly and started back felt as if it were going to tear him loose and hurl him outward like a projectile from a catapult.

He brought the binoculars up with both arms wrapped around the mast, and swept them along the line of the horizon off to port. At first he was afraid he'd waited too long. Then his pulse leaped. There she was, a minute sliver of white poised just over the rim of the world.

"If you're made fast down there," he called out, "one of you give me the heading."

"We can't see her from down here," the man yelled back.

"No. I mean our heading. How are we lying?"

The woman went aft and peered into the binnacle. "Two-nine-oh," she shouted up at him.

He looked down at the deck, estimating the angle on the bow. Call it four points, he thought. Forty-five from two-ninety left two-forty-five. *Saracen*'s bearing had remained practically unchanged from the first. Warriner was apparently headed for the Marquesas.

If he had thought to fool them by changing course after he was over the horizon, the chances were he would have already done it. *Orpheus,* with her bare masts, had long since dropped from sight from over there, and he'd probably assume he was equally invisible. Or would he? Just because he was unbalanced or mentally sick didn't mean he had to be stupid. Witness the story he'd made up about the deaths from botulism.

He put the glasses back to his eyes. The little point of white thinned and disappeared, then came up again. Was she still on there? What was happening now, or had happened already? He closed his eyes for an instant and prayed. When he opened them and looked through the glasses again, *Saracen* was gone over the curvature of the earth. He looked around at the slickly heaving, empty miles of the equatorial Pacific shimmering under the sun without even the suspicion of a breeze and felt sick. Automatically he glanced at his watch to note the time. It was 9:50.

[5]

FAR TO THE NORTHWARD A SQUALL FLICKERED AND RUMbled along the horizon, but here they appeared to hang suspended in a vacuum while the sun beat down and the oily groundswell rolled endlessly up from the south. The air was like warm damp cotton pressing in on them, muggy, saturated, unmoving. Perspiration didn't evaporate. It collected in a film over the body, a film that became rivulets, now running, now stopping momentarily, now moving again with the irritating feel of insects crawling across the skin. It ran down into his already sodden and clinging shorts and dripped into his sneakers. His back ached from crouching under the boom.

Dip, lift, throw—it went on without stop. The man was working silently above the after cabin, throwing water with a machine-like regularity now that matched his own, and he could hear the steady stream from the pump. It had been an hour and ten minutes since he'd come down from the mast. They'd thrown out nine to ten tons of water, at least, and still the buckets came up full. He'd made no attempt to get a sounding before they started; it was unnecessary. The problem was too elementary to need any measurements—either they got the water out of those cabins this way within a few hours or they were done. If it continued to rise, or even if it remained at the same level, they had no chance, because they obviously couldn't keep this up indefinitely. And whenever they stopped to sleep or collapsed from exhaustion, she'd go down.

He was dehydrated, and the ropy saliva inside his mouth tasted like brass. He wondered if they had fresh water that wasn't contaminated, and then remembered Warriner hadn't been suffering from thirst. Straightening, he looked aft. The woman was tiring; it was evident in the strained and set expression on her face. And the man, though there'd been no word of complaint, was in pain from the blow on his head. It showed in his eyes, below the level of that hard-boiled and half-contemptuous amusement with which he seemed to regard everything that happened.

He walked aft and took the pump handle. "Better take five," he said. "And get a drink. It's not going to help things if you keel over." He turned to the man. "You too."

"I'll bring some water," she said and went below. Ingram bent to the pump. In a moment she came back, carrying a saucepan full of water and a cup and a pack of cigarettes. She set the water on top of the doghouse, lit one of the cigarettes, and sat down on deck with her feet on the steps of the doghouse hatch. There was no protection anywhere on deck from the brutal weight of the sun, and the trapped air below would be stifling. The man took a drink and sat down on deck with his legs dangling in the hatch where he'd been working. After he'd had a cup of the water himself, Ingram went on pumping, driven by the compulsion to hurry, to do something, anything, and by fear of his thoughts if he stopped.

"How about one of your cigarettes, honey?" the man asked.

The woman tossed them toward him silently, without even looking at him. He lit one and asked Ingram, "How much gas you figure you had aboard?

Ingram continued to pump. "Maybe a hundred and fifty miles at normal cruising speed. Wide open, the way he left here, not much more than half of that—if he doesn't burn the engine up first."

"So call it a round hundred," the man said. "It's been a long time since I diddled around with the pi-r-square jazz, but won't that work out to a good-sized piece of ocean?"

"Yeah," Ingram replied. "With nothing else to go on, about thirty thousand square miles."

"I had a hunch you couldn't carry it around in a cup. And that's not to mention the fact he's not going to stop just because he runs out of gas. We get a breeze, he'll probably get one too. The wind blows on the nutty as well as the beautiful and the pure in heart. Shakespeare. Or was it Salmon P. Chase?"

"I said with nothing else to go on," Ingram pointed out curtly. "We know which way he left here, and it's almost a cinch he's headed for the Marquesas. That's the reason I went up the mast, to see if he'd changed course. He hasn't. And if we ever hope to make land, the Marquesas are the best chance we've got. So why not follow him? And see if we can keep this thing afloat? But don't let me influence you, if you've got a better suggestion."

The other shrugged. "Keep your hair on. I was just trying to estimate the chances. Not good, huh?'

"No," Ingram said. He was about to mention that they had one advantage in that Warriner would have to sleep sometime, but bit it back. It presupposed his being alone on *Saracen*.

The man glanced up as if he'd read his thoughts. "There were just the two of you?"

Ingram nodded.

"Naturally, you never know what a creep'll do, but she might have a chance. He likes a woman around to cry on."

Ingram wanted desperately to reach for this ray of hope, but he'd never been good at self-deception. "And go into port somewhere with a witness?"

"Golden Boy's not so hot at the long-range view. He might not think about that for days, especially with a nice bosom to throw himself on with his Kleenex."

"Will you, for Christ's sake, shut up?" the woman asked wearily.

Ingram glanced at her with curiosity, aware this was the first time he'd actually seen her since that first glance in the cabin, when his only impression had been that she was scared to death and appeared to be naked. Since he'd come back aboard he'd paid no attention to either of them except as to their potential value as tools or pieces of equipment in the matter of keeping this sodden tub afloat and following *Saracen* in it. She was probably in her late thirties, or perhaps even forty, but a strikingly handsome woman in spite of the disarray of her hair and the exhausted and sweat-streaked face. The hair itself was raven black except for a streak of gray, and the eyes were large and brown, but with more imperiousness than gentleness in them. She wore brief white shorts and a white halter which could have been a soiled gray and still appeared like snow against the tan of her body. Under other circumstances he might have noted that she had superb legs, but at the moment he was only wondering if she'd rested long enough to start pumping again. That, and what the hostility was between the two of them. Probably Warriner, he thought, remembering the way Rae had defended him. He seemed to have some fatal fascination for women older than himself. Rae was thirty-five. Then, for the first time, he remembered that presumably there'd been four people on here.

"What happened to Mrs. Warriner?" he asked.

The man grinned. "After marrying Hughie-boy, what *could* happen to anybody? It already has."

The woman exhaled smoke and looked musingly at Ingram. "I'd like to correct the impression you seem to have that I'm married to this specimen of *Pithecanthropus erectus*. I'm Mrs. Warriner."

He said nothing, but his surprise must have showed on his face, for she smiled a trifle wearily and said, "Yes, I am, aren't I?"

"Momma likes 'em young and mixed up," the man said, and Ingram decided today probably wasn't the first time he'd been slugged by somebody. Even people otherwise in full command of their faculties must have found the urge too much to resist.

He introduced himself and added, "We were bound from Florida to Papeete."

"I'm very glad to know you, Mr. Ingram," she said. "But sorry about the circumstances. This fringe-area human being is Mr. Bellew. If you've been wondering why my husband cracked up, perhaps the mystery is clearing. Just multiply your brief acquaintance by twenty-six days."

But there was still the fourth one. "And Mrs. Bellew?"

Bellew turned toward Mrs. Warriner, his eyes bright. "Why don't you tell him, honey? Nobody ever likes my version."

"Estelle drowned," she said. "Or was killed by a shark—"

"Or she was hit by a hockey puck, or some drunk in a sports car." Bellew took a final drag on his cigarette and dropped it between his knees into the water in the cabin. "Hughie-boy killed her."

"That's a lie!" Mrs. Warriner's voice was under control, but Ingram could see the fury in her eyes.

"Oh, not deliberately, perish the thought." Bellew looked at Ingram and made a deprecating gesture with his hands. "Hughie-dear wouldn't even dream of killing anybody—unless she happened to be in the way when he was trying to save his precious neck. Naturally, you can't have that sort of thing. What kind of world would it be without Hughie?"

"You were the one, if anybody was, you blind fool!" Mrs. Warriner started to get up, her self-control beginning to slip. "If you'd watched what you were doing—"

"Break it up!" Ingram's command cut through the scene with a parade-ground bark that halted her. "Both of you! You can fight some other time, if there is one. Get back to work."

With a venomous glance at Bellew, Mrs. Warriner took the pump. The other stood up and reached for the bucket. "And then Hughie hit this nasty old shark right on the nose, and he says you take that, you nasty old shark you. My wife can whip your wife."

Mrs. Warriner started to turn, her face pale. Ingram caught her arm and wheeled her back to the pump. At the same time he barked at Bellew. "Shut up and start throwing water!"

Bellew looked at him with lazy insolence for a moment, as though on the point of refusing out of mere curiosity as to what would happen. Then he shrugged and dropped the bucket through the hatch. "You might have a point there, sport. Drowning makes an awful mess of my hair."

Ingram returned to the hatch forward of the deckhouse, dropped the bucket, and began furiously throwing water overboard, conscious of the wasted minutes. What kind of madhouse was this? With the boat sinking under their feet, you had to tear them from each other's throats and drive them to make them try to save themselves. Well, they'd pump, God damn them; they'd pump till they were standing on their tongues.

What had happened to the fourth one, Estelle Bellew? At the moment he didn't care, but it was a way to keep from thinking of Rae. Didn't they even know? How could one call it an accident and the other say Warriner had killed her? Warriner was fleeing from something, there was no doubt, from some terror that had pushed him over the edge into madness. Or was he only running from Bellew? If you were weak and unstable to begin with, twenty-six days of Bellew's sadistic bullying and amused contempt would drive anybody around the bend. But why in the name of God had they ever started out together in the first place, to sail across the Pacific, four of them in an unsound boat? Well, they must have been friends then, friends and too lacking in experience to know what being cooped up on a small boat for weeks at a time could do to clashing personalities.

But it was futile. His thoughts always came back to the question from which there was no escape. What would Warriner do? But if he were insane, how could you even guess? Where did you start? Would he kill her or throw her overboard because she was a witness to the fact he'd gone off and left three people to drown on a sinking boat? Or worse, did he believe he'd killed Bellew? Presumably, he'd hit him from behind, and Bellew had fallen into the water, probably unconscious. Therefore Warriner might be convinced he was guilty of murder—in addition to whatever had happened to Estelle Bellew—and obviously there could be no turning back and no surviving witnesses. But this was assuming a mind at least partially capable of rational thought, of reasoning from cause to effect, from crime to punishment and how to escape it. Well, hadn't he already shown he was capable of that? He'd made up that very clever and very plausible story about the deaths from botulism just to keep him, Ingram, from going aboard *Orpheus* and discovering what he'd done. The answer probably was that there wasn't any answer, nothing ever clear-cut and definite; even the hopelessly psychotic must have rational intervals. Maybe at times he knew what he was doing, while at others he was completely cut off from reality.

Then what? Rae was no match for him physically; he was a powerfully built man in his early twenties. You could forget that. And there was no weapon— He stopped. The shotgun. It was a twelve-gauge double he'd brought along for hunting in Australia and New Zealand. But it was taken down, the barrels and stock wrapped separately in oiled sheepskin and stowed in a drawer where it could be sealed by customs in ports where it wasn't permitted. She knew nothing about guns; could she ever assemble and load it? No, that wasn't the question. Could she use it? Could she deliberately shoot a man with it? And if she did, what would it do to her afterward? There was nothing pretty about the results of a shotgun blast at close range; she'd have nightmares the rest of her life and wake up screaming— Stop thinking about things you have no control over, he told himself. That's out of your hands; just throw water and keep throwing it. It can't be running in as fast as we're dumping it out now; something's got to give.

It was less than thirty minutes later that two things happened almost at once. The first was a definite indication that they were gaining on the water: as it rushed from side to side with *Orpheus*'s rolling, the bucket would sometimes strike bottom and come up less than full. Maybe less than a foot deep in the cabins now, he thought, if she were on an even keel; they'd thrown out probably that much in an hour and a half of furious pumping and bailing. The other thing was a breeze.

He'd been so intent on bailing, his first awareness of it was the cool feel on his face. He looked up. It was straight out of the west, and as far as he could see the surface of the sea was wrinkled and dark. "Wind," Mrs. Warriner called out at the same moment.

"Right," he said. "Just keep pumping; you can take the wheel in a minute." He dropped the bucket and began casting the gaskets off the mainsail, working feverishly and praying the wind would last. He freed the end of the boom, took a strain on it with the topping lift, and re-shackled the halyard to the head of the sail. He hoisted it, tightened it down with the winch, and started on the double for the jib. Then he turned and called back to the other two, "Have you got a genoa aboard?" No doubt he'd regret it by the time he'd manhandled it from one side to the other a dozen times or so in these fluky airs, but every foot of distance was precious. A genoa would add almost the equivalent of another mainsail to her, and it was going to take all the canvas they could get on her to move this hulk in anything short of a gale.

It was Mrs. Warriner who replied, "Yes, there's a genoa, and also a big nylon spinnaker. The sail locker's forward. Do you want me to show you?"

"No. I'll get it." There was a hatchway to the forward cabin. He opened it and hurried down the ladder. The light was dim below deck, the air stifling and saturated with moisture, and water washed back and forth around his legs. In back of the ladder was a doorway opening into the locker in the bows of the boat. The sailbags were stowed in a bin on the port side, some six or eight of them altogether. He began muscling them out and looking at the markings on the sides. There were spare mainsails and mizzens, a couple of jibs, a storm trysail, a spinnaker, and the genoa jib. He looked at this young fortune in sails and wished they'd bought a hull to go with them.

He beefed the genoa back up the ladder, dumped it in the bow, and began unhanking the smaller jib. The breeze was still cool against his sweaty face, and *Orpheus* had begun to come ponderously up into the wind, still rolling heavily. He got the genoa snapped onto the stay, shackled the halyard to its head, and hoisted it. He didn't know where the sheet was, but grabbed up one of the lines littering the deck, made it fast to the clew, led it out around the port shrouds, through the block on the port side of the deck aft of midships, and back to the winch near the cockpit. *Orpheus* swung off to starboard. The mainsail filled, with the genoa aback and blown in against the shrouds. She began to move slowly ahead. When she had steerageway; he brought the wheel hard over; she came slowly up into the wind and fell off on the starboard tack with both the mainsail and genoa full and drawing. He checked the compass. They were heading 220. He came right a little and retrimmed the sheets, but 225 was the best they could do. It wasn't too far from the course they wanted.

He called out to Mrs. Warriner, "You take the wheel now. Bellew can relieve you there at the pump."

She came aft. Bellew moved to the pump, for once without comment. Ingram broke out the mizzen and hoisted it. The breeze had continued to freshen, and now tiny whitecaps were winking on the broad undulations of the swell. During all this burst of furious activity and the excitement of getting under way, the fear had been pushed to the back of his mind, but now as he looked over the side it all came back with a rush, along with a galling and futile anger. Were they moving at all? With the same breeze *Saracen* would have been footing along at four or five knots, but this sodden coffin had little more than steerageway.

"Let me take her again for a minute," he said to Mrs. Warriner. Maybe they were pinching her, trying to point higher into the wind than she would sail. She relinquished the wheel. He came aft ten degrees, started the sheets, retrimmed them, tried her farther off the wind, and came back. It was no use. She had no feel of life to her anywhere, no desire to move; she answered the helm with the leaden apathy of a dying animal that no longer wanted anything but rest.

He hadn't expected much, but this was even worse. If you could manufacture your own wind to order, by direction and force, you couldn't make fifty miles a day. He came back to the original course, turned the wheel over to Mrs. Warriner, stepped over the rail, and looked down. Below the waterline streamers of green hair wove backward with their passage. With ten to twenty tons of water inside her and that pasture on the bottom, he thought, how could you expect anything to move her? "When was the last time she was hauled out?" he asked Mrs. Warriner.

"About eight months ago," she replied. "When we bought her."

Well, that figured; it matched everything else about this expedition. He stepped down into the doghouse and dug a chart of the South Pacific out of the litter on the deck. Even if they weren't going anywhere, they had to have a position, a point of departure. Their last position should be in the logbook, but he didn't trust their navigation. He'd had a good fix from three star sights just at dusk last night; from that, by dead reckoning, they'd made twenty-five miles along a course of 235 degrees. That should be *Saracen*'s position at dawn when he'd sighted *Orpheus*. She was—call it five miles away, on a bearing of 315. That would put her here.

He penciled a cross on the chart: 4.20 South latitude, 123.30 West longitude. The Marquesas were roughly twelve hundred miles to the west southwest, the Galápagos over two thousand miles behind them, and elsewhere nothing but thousands of miles of empty ocean. The chances of their being sighted by a ship were to all practical purposes nonexistent.

And as for ever catching up with *Saracen,* even if they could find her . . . Face it, he thought. She was already far over the horizon, making six knots under power. And when her fuel ran out, she could still outsail this waterlogged hulk with nothing but her mizzen and somebody's shirt.

"The wind's heading us," Mrs. Warriner called out from the cockpit. He went back on deck. The breeze had veered around to the southwest, and she had bare steerageway on a course that was now a little east of south.

"We'll come about," he said. He cast off the genoa sheet, carried the sail forward around the stay and outside the starboard shrouds, and trimmed the sheet on the port tack. They were steering 275 now, which was 35 degrees to the west of the course they wanted. But in a few minutes the wind went further around to the southward and they were able to come down to 245. Then it died out momentarily and sprang up again out of the northwest. He carried the genoa around again. Ten minutes later the wind began to soften once more, and then died with complete finality. *Orpheus* slogged forward a few feet, came to rest, and began to roll heavily in the trough. He looked around the horizon. In every direction the surface of the ocean had the slick, hot glare of polished steel.

They'd made less than a mile. It was 12:10 p.m.

Her face hurt. It was lying on something hard that went up and down and wove back and forth the way the floor had the only time in her life she'd ever been drunk, and there was that same sick feeling in her stomach. Somewhere a long way off there was an engine sort of noise that seemed to have been going on forever, and just audible above it, or through it, a voice was singing. It was an old, very sentimental popular song, one she hadn't heard for years, but it was still familiar. What *was* it? Oh, "Charmaine." That was it. She rolled over. Some powerful light glared beyond her closed eyelids, and she grasped that it was sunlight. She opened them and squinted with pain. Just beyond her was a pair of wide and very sun-tanned shoulders surmounted by a gold-thatched head. At the same moment the head turned, still singing, and Hughie Warriner regarded her with concern, which gave way to evident relief. He smiled. It was a charming and affectionate smile, and there was something almost chiding about it. She tried to scream, or to move, but could do neither.

The song stopped. "See, you're all right," he said. "Now aren't you sorry you made me do it?"

[6]

JOHN WASN'T HERE. THE PARALYSIS OF SHOCK SNAPPED then, and she screamed. "Where are we? Where are you going? We've got to go back!"

Warriner gave no indication he'd even heard her. She

tried to sit up and was assailed by vertigo. The ocean tilted while nausea ballooned inside her, and she collapsed, fighting to keep from being sick. She closed her eyes for an instant to stop the whirling, and when she opened them Warriner had turned forward again to look into the compass. He was sitting in the helmsman's seat in the back of the cockpit, just beyond her legs. He reached a hand around and caught her left ankle, not tightly or roughly, but merely as though to soothe her or to reassure himself that she hadn't disappeared.

She cringed and tried to scuttle backward, but there was nowhere to go; behind her was only the sea. She was cut off; she couldn't reach the wheel or the ignition switch, or even the rest of the boat, without getting past him. There was nothing to hit him with, even if she had the strength.

The hand slid down her ankle and was caressing her bare foot. He turned around again. "You have such beautiful feet," he said. "And women so seldom do. I mean, they do to start with, but they ruin them. Especially European women."

She could only stare in horror.

"In fact, I've often wondered if Gauguin didn't run away to Polynesia simply because he was revolted by the feet of European models." His eyes sought hers in a glance that was amused and intimate, as though they shared some secret joke. "Of course it's silly. It's just something you say to clods at cocktail parties."

Dear God, how did you get through to him? "Listen!" She made it to a sitting position this time, lurched once as *Saracen* rolled, and caught herself with a hand on the lifeline. "Please! We've got to go back! Don't you understand? Turn around. Turn. Like this." She made a lateral motion with her free hand, as though trying to explain the mechanics of wheel-turning to an idiot or to someone who spoke another language. She realized immediately this was wrong, but was too frantic to know how to correct it. She went on, the words tumbling over each other in her haste. "Let me! Let me take it!"

"No." The smile disappeared. He gave a petulant little

shrug, as though she had disappointed him, and faced forward to stare into the binnacle again.

She turned and looked wildly astern. How far had they come? At first she couldn't even see the other boat and felt herself begin to give way to panic. Then she made it out, almost hull down on the horizon directly behind them. There was no chance at all of seeing the dinghy at that distance, and she didn't know what had become of John. Except that he wasn't here, and they were already nearly three miles away and going farther with every minute. She was the only chance he had. She turned back and caught Warriner's shoulder. "Go back! We've got to go back!"

He brushed her hand off. "Please, Mrs. Ingram, do you have to shout? You're being unreasonable again."

"Un—un— Oh, God!" She tried to calm herself; if she went to pieces she'd never get through to him. *"Unreasonable?* Can't you understand? My husband's back there. We can't go off and leave him. He'll drown."

Warriner dismissed the whole subject of Ingram with an abstracted wave of the hand. "He won't drown."

"But's the boat's sinking—"

"It probably won't. Anyway, he wanted to go aboard there, didn't he? It's his own fault." He turned and looked at her, as though puzzled by her refusal to grasp so obvious a fact. Then he went on, as if talking to himself. "My trouble has always been that I trust people too much. I don't see their real motives until too late. . . ."

It was hopeless, she realized then. Communication was impossible. Then what was left? Try to take the wheel away from him? Even in her desperation she realized the futility of that. And if she provoked him to violence again, this time he might kill her or throw her overboard. It wasn't fear of being hurt or even killed that made her rule that out, or reserve it as a final gamble when everything else had failed, but merely the simple, monolithic fact that her staying on here and staying alive represented the only chance they had. She had to try every other possibility first. But what? Then the answer occurred to her: she couldn't make him turn back, but at least she could stop his going any farther. It was still dead calm, and there was a good chance it would remain that way for hours, or even the rest of the day; if she could disable the engine, John might be able to reach them in the dinghy. But access to it was below; she had to get down into the cabin. Would he let her?

She pushed herself to her knees, grasping the lifeline, and made a tentative move to go past him along the deck on the starboard side of the cockpit. "I—I feel sick at my stomach," she said. "I've got to go to the head."

He gestured toward the rail. "Why not there?"

"I don't like being sick in public."

"No, of course not," he said sympathetically. "I'm sorry. I didn't think of that."

She wasn't conscious of the utter madness of this conversation until she was halfway down the ladder, and wondered if she was losing contact with reality herself. All the landmarks and reference points of rational existence had been so suddenly jolted out of position, she couldn't orient herself. It was as though they were threatened with destruction by the blind and impersonal trajectories of some hitherto placid machine that had run amok through a short circuit in its wiring. Warriner perhaps didn't intend any harm to either of them; they just happened to be in his path. Nor was he threatening her with violence or placing her under any restraint; she was merely powerless to do anything about him.

He couldn't see down into the cabin from where he was, in the aft end of the cockpit; once she was down the ladder she was out of sight. The engine was installed under the cockpit, and access to the compartment was through a removable panel in the after bulkhead of the cabin. She turned and was on the point of lifting the panel out when it occurred to her she had no idea at all what she was actually going to do. Disabling the engine had a fine sound to it—but just *how* did she disable it, and what was she going to do afterward?

The minute it stopped he would come hurrying down the ladder to find out what had happened. And even if she'd succeeded in sabotaging it beyond immediate repair it might be hours before John got here. It would be some time before he was sure *Saracen* had stopped, and it would take at least an hour to row a dinghy this far. She had to have some line of retreat, a place to barricade herself where Warriner couldn't reach her. The companion hatch itself couldn't be fastened from inside. The head? No, the door was too light. Warriner could smash the panel out of it with one kick. The forward cabin, that was the answer. The door was heavier and had a bolt inside. Also there were the cases of stores and the heavy sailbags to barricade it with.

Just hurry, she thought. She lifted the panel out and was assailed by sudden fear as the noise level, already high, increased. Would he notice it? She looked fearfully up at the hatch, expecting to see it darken. Nothing happened. Where he was sitting was almost above it; probably the difference in noise level was too small to be apparent up there. The compartment was dark, but there was a light switch just inside the entrance. She flicked it on and leaned in.

The engine had been running at nearly full throttle for a half-hour, and in addition to its ear-shattering racket the compartment was filled with the fumes of hot paint and burning oil. She felt nausea push up into her throat again. The engine itself was in the center of the small space, with the starting and lighting batteries on her right and a metal locker containing spare parts and tools on her left.

She studied it, searching for a vulnerable spot to attack. Though she had once been a sports-car enthusiast and had for a short period in her life owned an agency for one of the Euorpean cars, she knew little more about gasoline engines than does the average woman. She was aware, however, that they could be stopped by shutting off either the gasoline supply or the spark that exploded it. There was a valve in the small copper line coming from the fuel tank to the connection on the engine, but closing that would solve nothing. She could take a hammer from the toolbox and smash the line itself, but that would let the fuel drain into the bilges and convert the boat into a potential bomb. Then how about pulling loose a bunch of wires? That was better, but still not perfect. Warriner could replace them in less than an hour. Then her glance fell on the distributor. There was the answer. Smash that, and the power plant was permanently out of commission.

Then she had a better idea. Why not just remove the cap, where the wires came out? She could take it into the cabin with her; the engine couldn't run without it, and when John got aboard he could replace it and they'd still have the engine intact. She'd watched him take it off to clean the contacts and was certain she knew how to do it. All it required was pulling out those five wires and releasing the two spring clips on the sides, and then it lifted right off. But even that would take longer than the single hammer-blow it would require to smash it, and if he made it down here before she was locked in he would simply replace it after he'd taken it away from her. She paused, undecided, and was about to abandon the idea when another occurred to her.

How many times had John cautioned her never—no matter how short of space she was around the galley—to set anything on the ladder? To the person descending, it was invisible until he'd stepped on it and fallen. She whirled and reached into the stowage racks above the sink and brought out three saucepans. She set them in a row on the next-to-bottom step; under way, *Saracen* wasn't rolling heavily enough to throw them off within the next few minutes, which was all the time she needed.

She bent over and crawled into the compartment. With the metal locker pushing against her back and the bottom of the cockpit crowding her above, it was difficult to balance herself against the corkscrew motion of the boat's stern. Here right up against the engine the racket was deafening, and she could feel herself growing sick again from the fumes. She turned slightly, so as to be headed outward. Now—

She yanked out the wire in the center of the cap. The roar of the engine cut off abruptly. She began furiously snatching out the other four, the ones to the spark plugs. She had three of them loose and was reaching for the fourth when *Saracen* rolled down to port and she lost her balance. She fell over on the engine, her left forearm against the hot exhaust manifold. The sudden pain was too much for her already nauseated stomach. All the strength drained out of her and she collapsed, vomiting onto the floorboards beside the engine. Light footsteps sounded in the cockpit pressing against the top of her head.

Maybe even now there wasn't time to get out. But she had to have the cap; she'd never get another chance. She groped blindly for the last wire and had it in her hand when she was seized by another spasm of sickness. She tore it loose, still vomiting, and clawed at the spring clips on the side. The cap came free. She propelled herself toward the opening, and as her head emerged she saw Warriner's bare legs hurrying down the ladder, above her and to her right. She was cut off; she'd taken a second too long.

Then his right foot came down on the outer rim of one of the saucepans. It flew from under him and he landed amid a metallic crashing at the foot of the ladder. She was out of the engine compartment now, and if she could get by him before he got to his feet she might make it. As she shot past he threw out an arm and caught her ankle. She pulled free but was spun off balance, and she fell over against the port bunk. He had rolled over and was scrambling to his feet. She bounced off the bunk, somehow still clutching the distributor cap, and flung herself toward the entrance to the forward cabin. She was in. She slammed the door, but before she could throw the bolt he hit it from the other side.

It came inward. She had her shoulder against it, but her feet were slipping along the deck as she was forced back. Without something to brace herself against, the outcome was inevitable. She looked behind her and saw the piled sailbags on the port bunk just beyond her legs. Putting her right foot up against them, she managed to straighten the leg enough to lock her knee. It was impossible to force him back, but the door wasn't open enough for him to squeeze through. She could hear his feet sliding on the deck outside as he tried to get enough traction to bring his full strength to bear. A minute went by. She could feel herself growing faint, and her knee was beginning to tremble.

She still had the distributor cap in her hand and tried frantically to think of some way to dispose of it. Maybe she could toss it behind something. No. He knew she had had it when she ran in here; he'd find it, no matter what she did with it. But it was made of plastic; maybe if she slammed it down hard enough it would break. She shifted it to her free right hand and threw it with the last of her strength against the planking of the deck. It bounced upward at a slight angle, caromed off the sailbags, passed under her straining and almost horizontal body, and came down, spinning, near the bulkhead, less than a foot from the partially opened door, still intact. If he reached in he could pick it up.

He had never uttered a word. She could hear only his labored breathing and the scuffing of his sneakers against the deck on the other side of the door, and the decreasing sounds of water going past the hull as *Saracen* slowed and came to rest. There was a quality of horror somehow in this very absence of speech that made her shiver. She couldn't hold out much longer; her leg was going to buckle any second.

She threw herself suddenly to the left, releasing the door. It flew inward, and he shot past her, losing his balance and falling to the deck between the bunks. She scooped up the distributor cap and ran through the after cabin toward the ladder. If she could only make it into the open before he caught her she could throw it overboard. Her head and shoulders were above the hatch, and she was drawing back her arm to throw it, when she was caught from below. It dribbled out of her hand and into the bottom of the cockpit. She managed to kick free, ran up the last two steps, and leaped into the cockpit after it. She had it in her hand when his weight landed on her from behind and she was slammed down on the port seat of the cockpit with the hand pinned beneath her body.

But he made no effort to reach beneath her and pull it out; his hands were digging at the back and sides of her neck as he tried to close his fingers around her throat. She hunched her shoulders up and pulled her chin down, grinding her face against the cushion. Then his weight was suddenly gone from her shoulders and she was lifted and thrown onto her back. She kicked out with her legs and struck at his face, but his hands were around her throat now and tightening. The contorted face and wild eyes were just above hers, and she closed her own eyes to shut them out.

The struggle was utterly silent except for a faint whining sound he made deep in his throat and the sibilant whisperings of their violence against the plastic cushion. She could no longer breathe, and the sunlight penetrating her closed eyelids began to fade downward through darkening shades of pink toward final blackness. But her hand was free now. Just as consciousness was slipping away she raised it and threw the distributor cap outward. There was no sound of its striking the deck, so it must have gone into the water. Or maybe she was already beyond hearing. . . .

Then, strangely, she was breathing again. The hands were gone from her throat. She opened her eyes. He had stood up and was leaning across her, with his hands on the port lifeline, as though he'd forgotten her. She couldn't see his face. She slid cautiously backward, toward the forward end of the cockpit. He paid no attention. She eased herself upright, poised to leap toward the hatch, and glanced fearfully once more in his direction to see if he had turned. This time she saw his face and understood. She looked outward in the same direction.

It was the distributor cap. It had landed just off the port side, and with *Saracen* now lying at rest on the surface it was sinking almost straight below them through sunlit water as clear as gin. And as he had the other time at the bottle, he was staring down at it with horror and with some sick but inescapable compulsion as it slipped from side to side and then began a gentle spiral that would end in the ooze and the darkness two miles below. The agony of his face was indescribable. He screamed then and collapsed into the bottom of the cockpit with his face pressed into the seat cushion.

She stared, still poised to leap but frozen to the spot.

His head rocked from side to side and he clutched the cockpit coaming with a grip that corded the muscles of his forearms. "No, no, no!" he cried out. "I didn't do it! I didn't mean it! It was her fault!" He began to cry then with a ragged sobbing that made his whole body shake.

She was able to move at last. She ran down the ladder on rubbery legs and through the after cabin. After slamming the door between the two, she threw the bolt and began dragging cases of canned stores from under the bunks and piling them in front of it. There were six sailbags. She stacked them against the door also, wedging the last ones against the upright pipes of the bunk frame. She was trembling and drenched with perspiration when she had finished, and collapsed on the bunk, too weak to move. Her face was swollen and painful where he had hit her, and there was an ugly red splotch on the bottom of her left forearm where it had come in contact with the exhaust manifold. She was scared, and she was sick with anxiety for John, but for the moment she was safe. Without an ax to smash the door, Warriner had little chance of breaking in, and there was no ax aboard. And until they got a breeze he couldn't take *Saracen* any farther away. All she could do now was wait it out.

Saracen rolled desolately in the trough of the swell. There was no sound from beyond the door except the normal creakings, slidings, and minute collisions of shifting objects always present on a small boat at sea, and Rae might even have been alone. She tried to make some sense of this thing that had happened to them, but ran immediately into the opaque and impenetrable wall of the fact that Warriner was the only clue to any of it, and Warriner was mad. Where did you go from a starting point like that?

John had suspected there was something wrong with him. If only she'd paid more attention and hadn't waked him up by starting the engine . . . Well, there was no use crying about that now. But what had John found on the other yacht that had made him burst out of the cabin that way and leap down into the dinghy? Somebody hurt or sick? But in that case why was he coming back alone?

Wait, she thought, you're close. What he found must have been some proof Warriner was lying, unstable, or dangerous, or all three, and he was rushing back because you were alone here with him. But *what* proof?

Warriner had tried to kill her; maybe he'd already killed somebody else. It was abundantly obvious now he hadn't been chasing her to recover the distributor cap; the chances were he hadn't even known she had it. He'd been intent simply on strangling her because she'd somehow stopped the engine. And his horror at watching it sink had nothing to do with its being a part of the engine; he probably hadn't even recognized what it was. It was the same as with the bottle: he was seeing something else, or somebody.

I didn't do it! . . . I didn't mean it! . . .

Guilt? Terror? Who knew, or could even guess? But the whole story of the deaths from botulism must have been a lie, so it was possible something else and equally terrible had happened. Maybe he was responsible for it— She tensed. He was coming through the after cabin. She sat up and drew back on the bunk, waiting for the impact as he slammed into the door. Would it hold?

Then she grabbed her temples and fought a collapse into hysteria. He'd knocked—a tentative and discreet rap of the knuckles—and said forlornly, "Mrs. Ingram?"

You're not mad, are you, Mama? I didn't know it would hurt the cat. Stop it! she thought. You're beginning to crack up yourself.

He knocked again. "Mrs. Ingram? Please, I didn't mean it! You've got to believe me! I—I just lost my head for a minute, because I thought you were against me too. But you're not, are you? You couldn't be. You're like Estelle. The first minute I saw you, I could *feel* you talking to me, the way she did. Mrs. Ingram, what's your first name?"

She could only feel of her throat and go on staring at the door.

"Mrs. Ingram?"

She couldn't be sure, but she thought he was crying. Then in a minute he said petulantly, "Well, you *were* being unreasonable, you know. It was your own fault."

He turned the handle of the door and pushed, and when it failed to open he began to lunge at it in rage, like a child in a tantrum. She watched the bolt in horror, expecting to see it torn off, but it continued to hold. "You want to kill me too, don't you?" he shouted.

Then, as suddenly as it had commenced, the fury subsided. His footsteps went away.

She heard him moving around in the after cabin, and after a while the sound of hammering. It was impossible to guess what he was doing, but at least he wasn't trying to smash down the door. Would John have decided by now that *Saracen* was stopped? Maybe he was already heading for them in the dinghy. She looked at her watch. It was 9:35. He could probably row it in an hour, or maybe even a little less.

But suppose something had happened to him back there when he'd tried to get back aboard? The last she'd seen of him, just before Warriner hit her, he'd been coming toward them as hard as he could row, directly in their path. No, you had to have something to hang onto or you'd go as mad as Warriner, and faith in John Ingram's ability to cope with anything that could happen at sea was the one solid thing in sight. Even if he'd been run down, he would have got back aboard the other yacht, and he'd have the dinghy with him. And if the other yacht were sinking, he'd keep it afloat somehow—

Her thoughts broke off and she looked around in wonder. It was the growl of the starter she'd heard. Hadn't he even looked at the engine? Didn't he know the distributor head was gone? The engine fired then and settled down to a steady rumble. She heard the clutch engage, and they began to move ahead.

She slumped forward with her face in her hands and wanted to give up and cry. She'd never thought to look in the spare-parts box to see if there was another one. She should have known. John detested engines, but he always said that if you were going to carry the stinking things around they might as well be in working condition when you needed them.

[7]

HE'D ACQUIRED HIS FIRST CATBOAT AT THE AGE OF TWELVE, and, except for two years at the University of Texas on the GI Bill just after World War II, he'd been around salt water and around boats ever since, most of his adult life as a professional. He'd captained a towboat in Mexico, worked on salvage jobs in half a dozen countries and three oceans, owned and skippered a charter yacht in the Bahamas, and up until eighteen months ago operated a shipyard in Puerto Rico. He'd been in an explosion and fire, and inevitably he'd seen bad weather and some that was worse, but at the moment he didn't believe he'd ever been in a position quite as hopeless as this.

It was 2:45 p.m. Wearing a diving mask, he was some ten feet below the surface on *Orpheus*'s port side, just in under the turn of her bilge, looking at her from below, and the view was a chilling one. She'd never make port. And their pumping and bailing would accomplish nothing except to postpone from one hour to the next the moment she'd finally give up and go to the bottom.

When the breeze had stopped, they'd all three returned to throwing water out of her. Twenty minutes ago, after over an hour's furious and unceasing effort, they had lowered the water level in the main cabin to a depth of around six inches. Their bailing buckets were coming up less than half full each time. He'd knocked the others off for a brief rest and questioned them. Had they hit anything? Driftwood, or a submerged object of any kind? In mid-Pacific, this was admittedly far-fetched, but there had to be some reason for all that water.

It was Mrs. Warriner who supplied most of the answers. "No," she said. "If she did, we didn't feel it."

"When you were running on power, was there any unusual vibration?" If they had a damaged propeller or bent shaft she might have opened up around the stern gland.

Mrs. Warriner shook her head. "No, it was perfectly normal. Anyway, we haven't used the engine in over two weeks."

"We used up all the gas trying to find Clipperton Island," Bellew said. "Prince Hughie the Navigator knew where it was, but somebody kept moving it."

She gave him an icy stare but was too exhausted to reply. "How about bad weather?" Ingram asked.

There hadn't been much, at least nothing to bother a sound boat. Two days out of La Paz they'd run into a freak condition of fresh to strong winds which had kept them reefed down for the better part of twenty-four hours. They'd had a couple of days of bad squalls, the worst of which was around two weeks ago when they were trying to beat their way back to Clipperton Island after they'd decided they'd overshot it. The squalls had left a rough, confused sea, and she'd pounded heavily.

"And it was just after that you noticed it was taking more pumping to keep her dry?"

Mrs. Warriner nodded. "I think so. But it wasn't all of a sudden. Just a little more each day. And it must have been about three days ago it began to get really bad and come above the cabin floor when she rolled."

"How was the weather then?"

She thought. "Nothing stronger than light breezes, as I recall. But the day before was squally and rough, and she pitched quite a bit."

Ingram nodded and spoke to Bellew. "When you get your breath, turn to on the pump. I'm going below to see what I can find, and I'll relieve you in half an hour."

He was going through the doghouse when the thought of Rae poured suddenly through the defenses of his mind again, leaving him shaken and limp. No matter how you barricaded yourself against the fear, it lurked always in ambush just beyond conscious thought, ready to catch you off guard for an instant and overwhelm you. What chance did she have? Did she have any at all? Lay off, he told himself savagely; you'll run amok. Do what you can do and quit thinking about what you can't.

Below, in the sodden ruin of the cabins, he'd checked the obvious things first, all the plumbing leading through the hull below the waterline. There were two heads. He couldn't get a good look at the pipes because of the water swirling around them, but he could feel them with his hands. He wasn't looking for a minor leak, but a flood. They were all right; none of them were broken. He crawled through a hatch into the flooded engine compartment under the doghouse. The big two-hundred-horsepower engine was submerged to its rusty cylinder head in oily water surging from side to side. He groped around for the intake to the cooling system and examined the line with his hands. It was intact. Then the leaks had to be in the hull itself—God alone knew where—and there was no way to find them unless you could get her dry inside so you could look.

But you couldn't lower the water with the pump alone, and the buckets were useless after you got it as low as the cabin sole. Maybe there was a fire ax or hatchet aboard; he could chop away the cabin flooring below those two hatches and drop the buckets directly into the bilge. His eyes had grown accustomed to the dim light in the compartment now, and he looked around him, studying as much of the hull as was above the water. She was double-planked; he could see the diagonal seams of the inner skin. He took out his knife and began poking it at random into the wood. On the third plank the knife blade went into it as if it were a piece of bread. He felt a chill along the back of his neck and hurriedly started checking everywhere he could reach, even into the water below him. Large areas of the inner planking and of the frames themselves were spongy with dry rot.

He'd gone back on deck then and asked if there was a diving mask aboard. Mrs. Warriner told him where to find one. After kicking off his sneakers, he'd tossed the end of a line over the port side so he could get back aboard, and dropped in.

How long? he wondered now, peering upward through

the mask. It was impossible to guess; too much depended on the weather. In the first hard squall she'd go to the bottom like a dropped brick. In at least three places just above him along the turn of the bilge where the green hair of marine growth waved endlessly as she rolled, he could see the loose butt-ends of planks sticking out where her fastenings had worked loose. Around them the calking was gone, the seams wide open for the full length of the plank. Keeping a respectful distance from the plunging and deadly mass above him, he swam to the surface and forward, around the bow. The starboard side was even worse. He counted six planks where the fastenings were coming out. He swam back and climbed aboard.

Bellew stopped pumping, and they came over to him as he stood dripping on deck under the brazen weight of the sun. "Did you find anything?" Mrs. Warriner asked.

He stripped off the mask and nodded. "Yes. But it's nothing we can do anything about."

"Then she's going down?"

"Yeah. I wouldn't even make a guess as to how long we can keep her afloat, but she'll never make the Marquesas."

"What's causing it?" Bellew asked.

"Dry rot. In the inner planking and some of the frames. It's a disease, generally caused by lack of ventilation, and once it starts it spreads like smallpox. There may have been only a few small patches of it when you bought her, but whoever surveyed her missed 'em apparently, and now it's everywhere. What's happening is that, even if the outer planking is still sound, the fastenings are pulling out; the wood inside is too soft to hold 'em any more. Pounding in those squalls probably started them working loose, and now just the rolling sets up enough play and enough stresses to pull them out. The inner planking's no doubt opening up the same way, and the more she works, the looser it all gets."

"And there's nothing we can do?" Mrs. Warriner asked.

"Nothing except keep pumping."

She sat down at the break of the raised deck and lit a cigarette. She blew out the match and tossed it overboard.

"I'm sorry, Mr. Ingram. It's too bad we had to infect you."

Still occupied with the practical problem of survival, and its vanishing possibility of solution, he was caught off guard by this lapse into the figurative. "Infect?"

"With our own particular dry rot. Our contagion of doom. We should have been flying a quarantine flag."

Bellew had glanced involuntarily toward the dinghy still bumping against the side. Ingram saw him but didn't even bother to speak; he merely shook his head. Twelve hundred miles from land, three people in an eight-foot dinghy designed to carry two the hundred yards or so from an anchored yacht to the dock, inside a harbor—a bicycle would be about as practical a lifeboat.

Bellew shrugged. "So it was stupid." Then he went on, his eyes bleak. "But I guess you die hard, with unfinished business."

"Who doesn't?" Ingram asked.

"Sure, sure, you'd like to know what happened to your wife. Me, I'd just like two or three minutes with Hughie-boy." He raised brutal hands and made a twisting motion with them, inches apart. Mrs. Warriner sickened and turned away in a silence that seemed almost palpably to echo with the creak and snap of parted vertebrae. Ingram felt sorry for her. "Never mind," he said harshly to Bellew. "Get back to pumping."

The other fell to without reply. As though conscious of them now only for the first time, Ingram looked at the bull neck and massive shoulders and arms, thinking that Bellew probably could kill a man with his bare hands. It was a good thing he'd got the jump on him to start with. Or had he? It was impossible to tell what Bellew thought, or why he took orders without argument. He had the look of a man it would be very dangerous to push, and the chances were this docility under curt commands was nothing but a realistic acceptance of the facts that Ingram knew the job better than he did and he had more chance of saving himself if he did as he was told.

Ingram sat down in the cockpit to put his sneakers back on. Water still dripped from his hair. Mrs. Warriner sat facing him, on the edge of the raised deck, her knees drawn up, moodily smoking. "What is your wife like?" she asked.

"Why?" He didn't like the question; he saw no reason he should discuss Rae with these people.

"If she knows how to handle him, I don't think he'll hurt her."

"I'd like to believe that," he said bluntly. "But do you mean you *didn't* know how to handle him? When I opened the cabin door down there and you thought it was him, you were scared to death."

The brown eyes met his with perfect frankness. "The circumstances are different. He thinks we're trying to kill him. Also, it wasn't myself I was afraid for."

Ingram nodded, remembering how Bellew had been poised with his club. At the same time, something else disturbed him. Presumably that was her cabin, hers and Warriner's. Then if Warriner was on deck taking his trick at the pump when he'd sighted *Saracen,* why had Bellew been in there? But maybe Warriner had attacked him somewhere else and dragged him in there while he was unconscious. He shrugged. What difference did it make?

"Would she panic easily?" Mrs. Warriner asked.

"No," Ingram said. "I don't think she'd panic at all. Look, she's no high-school girl, or jittery old maid with the vapors. She's thirty-five years old, and she was married twice before she married me. Men are nothing new and startling to her. She's never had to deal with an unbalanced one before, but she *has* been in tight spots, and she's clever and coolheaded and she learns fast. She tried to fight him to get back to the wheel when he took it away from her, but all that happened very fast and it was pure reflex. If she survived—" His voice broke off, and he pulled savagely at the shoelace he was knotting. "If she survived that time, she'd know better than to antagonize him again. She'd play it by ear."

"Is there a weapon of any kind aboard?"

He nodded. "A shotgun."

Their eyes met again. Then she shivered slightly and

looked down at the cigarette in her hands. Her voice was very small as she asked, "Could she?"

"I don't know," he said. "Does anybody, till he's faced with it?"

"Is she aware that *Orpheus* is sinking?"

"All she knows is that there was water in her, and that your husband said she was. She won't know what to believe now."

"But the possibility—or probability—will still exist. So they'd be going off and leaving you to drown." She was silent for a moment. "Have you been married long?"

"About four months. We were on our honeymoon."

She nodded. "I can only give you the opinion of another woman who was, in effect, on her honeymoon. Both alternatives are impossible, of course, as long as you continue to weigh them. But inevitably there'll be a point when she has to stop thinking, and it'll become a simple matter of instinct versus conditioning. Instinct is a lot older."

"She may not even remember the gun. Or know how to assemble it if she does—or get the chance, for that matter."

"But she would know better than to try to threaten him with it? You know, the magic wand of television and B pictures?"

"Yes," he said. "She'd know better than to point it unless she was prepared to shoot it." He closed the discussion abruptly and stood up to look down the hatch. There was perceptibly more water in the after cabin than there had been thirty minutes ago. He motioned for Bellew to relinquish the pump.

"I'll take over for a couple of hours. We can't all work all the time, and I want to get some idea how fast it's rising against pumping alone. So the two of you'd better turn in on the settees in there and see if you can get some sleep. You're going to need it."

"Right," Bellew agreed. He started down the steps into the doghouse. Then he turned and asked, "How did he sucker you?"

Ingram explained briefly how Warriner had rowed out and come aboard, and the story he'd told. "It kept bothering me, especially his not wanting to come back aboard here or even wanting me to. But I had no real reason to doubt him, so I couldn't very well force him to, and I didn't like the idea of leaving my wife on there alone with him until I knew more about him. Then he turned in, and I decided to have a look anyway. But apparently he wasn't asleep. You didn't even know he'd left?"

"No," Bellew said. "When we heard you walking around, we thought it was still him. We didn't know he'd sighted a rescue boat when he slugged me and locked us in there. A laugh a minute, that Hughie-boy. Like to run into him again some day."

The contempt in Mrs. Warriner's voice was like a whiplash. "Are you sure that's why he hit you?"

"Why else, baby?" Bellew turned and went on below.

Ingram shrugged and began pumping. Mrs. Warriner remained where she was, turning slightly so she faced him. "I'm not sleepy," she said. "Do you mind if I talk?"

"Go ahead," he said.

She took a drag on her cigarette and stared moodily at the smoke. "I can understand your not wanting to talk about your wife under these circumstances—and least of all to me. But I'm trying to form a picture of her. Not to belabor the obvious any more than we have to, she's the key to this, naturally; we know what's going to happen on here, so if there is to be any other outcome it would have to hinge on what happens on there within the next few hours. You said she was thirty-five, which implies—or should imply—a certain amount of maturity. Is she pretty?"

"Yes," Ingram said. "She's very pretty."

Her smile was fleeting and faintly tinged with sadness. "It *was* a silly question to ask a bridegroom. Is she blond or brunette?"

"Blond," he said, still pumping. "Or in that jurisdiction. Her hair's somewhere between golden blond and light brown—tawny, I think you'd call it—and the eyes are sea-green. High cheekbones, very smooth complexion, beautiful tan. Generally speaking, it's the type of face and coloration that go with high spirit and a very low flashpoint in the temper department, but she grew up faster than the temper did, and somewhere along the line they gave her a sense of humor. Maybe she needed it, to marry me."

"Don't add too much modesty to your other virtues," she said. "It'll sound phony. Does she have any children?"

"No. She had a boy, but he died. Polio."

"I'm sorry. That was the first marriage?"

"The second. The first marriage was one of those kid things, during the war. That is, the Second World War—"

"Thank you, Mr. Ingram. But I know which one you mean. Go on."

"She wasn't quite seventeen, and he was a navigator in the Eighth Air Force. After the war he went back to school on the GI Bill, pre-med student. She worked, and they lived in a Quonset hut—you remember the routine. They were both too young for it, I guess; anyway, he was failing all his subjects and they began to fight and it didn't last. She went back to Texas, and they were divorced. The second marriage was another thing. No divorce; he was killed in an airplane crash."

"How old would the boy be if he'd lived?"

"Around twelve, I think."

"Does she attract children?"

"I don't know," he said. "I've never seen her around any."

"How about the lost, the insecure, the dependent, the scared?"

He saw the shadow of pain in her eyes again and knew what she meant. "She has a great deal of tenderness and sympathy," he said. "I don't know how apparent it'll be after she's just been slugged—"

"He'll know, don't worry. It's like radar. And he brings it out if it's been latent for years. With that, plus a reasonable amount of intelligence, I think she can handle him, provided she doesn't panic."

"Why does he think you tried to kill him?"

"He thinks Bellew and I are lovers. And that we planned to do away with him and Estelle." She made no attempt to look away. The brown eyes were completely without expression now, however, and he could only guess at the torment behind them. "Unfortunately, there is some justification for his thinking so. And it's my fault. I blamed the whole thing on Bellew awhile ago, but that was in anger. I'm probably as much responsible for his crackup as Bellew is, in a different way."

Ingram was beginning to like her and found that difficult to believe. Maybe she was too accustomed to taking the rap for everything; Warriner had struck him as an alibi artist who'd load it on anybody in sight. "Well, look, your husband's a grown man, or supposed to be—"

"The type of woman he attracts, or is attracted to, never give him a chance to be one. And it's too late now."

"What happened?" Ingram asked.

For a moment he thought she hadn't heard. Then she said, "That's a good question, and I wish I could answer it. Specifically, what happened was a very tragic accident. The accident itself is difficult enough to explain, but to understand why it smashed him you'd have to go back a long way. When was the first time, Mr. Ingram, that you realized it was possible for this environment of ours to be unfriendly, and that it was also possible to find yourself utterly alone in it? I mean, with nobody to take your head in her lap and tell you everything was going to be all right, that the critics were wrong, that the bank must have forgotten to credit your last deposit, that the pathologist must have made a mistake, or the teacher that gave you a D was just being spiteful?"

"I don't know," Ingram replied. "Probably a long time ago."

"Precisely. While you were still quite young, and under relatively harmless circumstances, and over the years you built up—well, not an immunity, nobody's immunized—but call it a progressively higher threshold of susceptibility. It happened to Hughie for the first time at the age of twenty-eight, alone in the middle of the Pacific Ocean without even a lifebelt, and he was there because he'd been betrayed by the one person he'd been conditioned all his life to trust and depend on—his mother, in one of her successive manifestations."

"Aren't you riding yourself pretty hard?" Ingram asked.

"No. I don't think so." She gazed out across the metallic glare of the sea to where the sun had already begun its descent into the west. "If you know the conditions when you accept the appointment, you also accept the responsibility. I let him down."

[8]

SHE WAS SILENT FOR A MOMENT. HOW DID YOU EXPLAIN Hughie to a man who'd seen only the wreckage after he'd been shattered by the Pacific Ocean, by Bellew's contemptuous bullying, and by her own misguided attempts to help him? How make him see the wit, the charm, the sensitivity, the genuine talent behind the beach-boy good looks?

Strangely enough, when she'd first met Hughie, a little over a year ago, he'd been living on a yacht. It was on the island of Rhodes, snuggled up under the Turkish coast on almost the opposite side of the world from where she was now, and the yacht, a glittering and obviously expensive yawl registered under the Panamanian flag, appeared to be more or less permanently moored in that harbor astride whose entrance the Colossus had towered two thousand years before. Hughie was living aboard it alone, and he was painting.

Oh, it wasn't his yacht, it belonged to a friend who was only letting him live on it, he'd disclaimed with a refreshing and boyish honesty that couldn't help appealing to a woman who'd known her share of phonies on two continents. It wasn't until somewhat later—too late, in fact—that she learned his frankness had been a little less than complete, that the friend was female, a wealthy American divorcée living in Rome, and that Hughie's relationship to her was one for which "protégé" was as good a euphemism as any. By that time she was—as she would have put it if she'd still been in any condition to view the thing with her old self-honesty and clarity of thought—hooked herself.

She saw him as a talented but too-beautiful boy who was being ruined by a continuously self-renewing matriarchy of lionizing sponsors, benefactresses, patronesses-of-art-at-the-source, surrogate mothers, and rapaciously protective beldames who started out wanting to adopt him and wound up by sandbagging him with the flushed and hectic urgencies of some autumnal reflowering and dragging him off to bed. And by the time she should have begun to suspect the weakness in his character she had made the further discovery that he wasn't a boy at all, that he was twenty-seven instead of the twenty she had thought, and she was hopelessly in love with him.

She was forty years old then and widowed nearly two years, no longer a victim of the grief and numbness of loss but only of its emptiness, the feeling that she must have been left over for something if she could only discover what it was. She'd come to Europe again. Since she belonged to a set to which the jet flight across the Pole was only a commute hop, she had friends in London, Paris, Antibes, Florence, and God knew where else, but she had avoided them, going on instead to Istanbul and then back to Athens and Corfu and a footloose and unscheduled wandering through the Dodecanese, searching for she knew not what. She'd arrived in Rhodes around the middle of July for a four-day stay. She'd met Hughie, and the four days had become a week, and then two, and finally a month.

"He's a painter," she went on. "A good one. And, given a chance, he might have become a great one. It wasn't his fault that women could never leave him alone—"

"If I'm not mistaken," Ingram broke in, "*nothing* is ever Hughie's fault."

She nodded somberly. "To some extent, that's true—if oversimplified. But there are reasons for it."

"I'm not knocking it. Probably a very comforting philosophy, as long as you can keep from having to sign for the mess sometime when there's nobody around to hand it to."

"It's the way he was raised," she said. "He's never had a chance. Even his childhood was against him. He's seen his father only once, and very briefly, in the past seventeen years. Though he's never said so directly, I gather he either hated him or was afraid of him, and probably at least some of it must have been his mother's fault. Certainly the picture that comes through from the few things he has said is one of such utter crudity and brutality it seems a little too one-sided to be quite true..

"His father was—or is, rather—the editor and publisher of a small daily newspaper in Mississippi, an ex-football player at one of the Southern universities, and from all accounts a man whose only passions apparently were drinking, random and indiscriminate affairs with very sordid women, white supremacy, and shooting quail. That plus bullying Hughie because the boy showed more interest in sketching animals than in killing them. It could be that all of this is literally true, in spite of its familiarity, but I wouldn't discount the possibility of a certain amount of editing by the doting mother and embittered ex-wife. At any rate, when Hughie was eleven his parents separated and were later divorced. His mother, who had a little money of her own, took him to Switzerland. He went to a private school in Lausanne but lived with her all the time in the villa she rented there so they wouldn't be separated. She never remarried. You can see the pattern, of course, the possessiveness, the overprotection, the you'd-never-leave-Mumsy-would-you-after-all-she's-done-for-you rubbish. After the school in Switzerland he attended the Sorbonne for two years and then began studying art, also in Paris, and also still living with his mother. She died five or six years ago. There was a little money left, but not enough to keep him going until he could get some kind of recognition as a painter. However—" She smiled with a tinge of bitterness, and went on. "Europe is crawling with middle-aged women eager to help the struggling young artist, especially if he's charming and decorative and well mannered and has no social liabilities like cutting off his ears or wasting too much time painting."

She broke off then with an impatient gesture, as though

annoyed at herself. "I'm sorry. You asked me about the accident. As I said, it's difficult to explain how it could have happened. Fortunately you know the interior layout here, which will help. Hughie and I occupied the after cabin, and Mr. and Mrs. Bellew the forward one—"

Ingram interrupted. "But first, who is Bellew, anyway? Somehow, I don't place him in this. Is he a friend, or a neighbor of yours in Santa Barbara?"

"I'm not from Santa Barbara," she replied. "San Francisco. We just bought the boat in Santa Barbara and sailed from there in the beginning." She shook another cigarette out of the pack and held the latter up toward Ingram at the pump.

"No, thanks," he said.

"You don't smoke?"

"Only cigars." He wished he had one, but among the other things he was wishing for at the moment it didn't have a very high priority. "But about Bellew?"

"He's a writer." Then, catching Ingram's look of surprise, she smiled faintly. "No, he *doesn't* remind you a great deal of Proust or Henry James. He's a specialized type of writer; he does articles for outdoor magazines. Hunting and fishing."

"Wait." Ingram frowned. "Bellew? Russell Bellew? I think I've seen some of his stories. Marlin fishing, and hunting sheep in Mexico. With some beautiful photography, as I recall."

"His wife did the photography. She was an artist with a camera."

Ingram stopped pumping for a moment and walked past her to the open hatch to look down into the cabin. In spite of his continuous pumping, the water was still rising. His face was somber as he walked back to the pump.

She lit the cigarette and carefully blew out the match. "Still gaining?" she asked.

"Yes," he said. She was a cool one, he thought; and so, for that matter, was Bellew. That was something, anyway; at least he didn't have a couple of screamers on his hands. Of course there was no telling how they'd take it later on.

But then, he added grimly, there was no telling how he'd do, either; it was something you couldn't forecast.

"But we can still hold it by bailing too, can't we?"

"Yes," he replied. "We can now."

"But not for long?"

"Just how long, I don't know. The only thing that's certain is that it's not going to get any better, but it *is* going to get progressively worse, with this rolling. And in a bad squall, as I told you, she could come apart like a bale of shingles. But forgetting the squall, which we can't do anything about anyway, she might last for a week yet. . . ." His voice trailed off.

She glanced up questioningly. "There's something else?"

There was no reason to try to hide it from her, he thought. "Only this—even if we do keep her afloat for another week, after tonight, or tomorrow morning at the latest, it's not going to do any good anyway. There's not a chance in a million we'll be sighted by a ship, not where we are. And even if one happened to pick us up on radar, there's nothing to indicate we're in distress.

"So, as you said, the only thing that could change it is if Rae is still on there and is able to cope with your husband. She might even be able to talk him into coming back. If she does, we'll probably be all right. The second possibility is that she may be able to get control of the boat some way. He'll have to sleep sometime, or . . ." He stopped, floundering.

She nodded, her face devoid of expression. "Or she may kill him. Go on."

If she could manage it, he could too. "Right," he said just as calmly. "But even if she does get control of the boat, it's nowhere near as simple as it sounds. She may never find us again. They're over the horizon now, and unless she knows the course he was steering when he left here, she can't come back because she won't know which way *back* is. Also, at the speed they were going, somewhere around midnight tonight and about a hundred miles from here they're going to run out of gas, and she can't make it back unless she gets some wind. In these conditions, it could take days. Also, at that distance, the accumulated errors of trying to make good a course while she's fighting fluky breezes and calms become so great that after a while she won't know within twenty miles where she is herself."

"She can't call for help, to get a search organized, even if there was anybody out here to look. We've got a radiotelephone, but it won't reach land from here, and you can't call a ship with it because they stand their radio watches on five hundred kilocycles and not the phone bands.

"So if she ever finds us again it'll be within the next twelve hours or so, because if they get any farther away there's practically no chance. Have you got any distress flares aboard?"

"No," she said. "We thought we had a can of them but we've never been able to find them."

"How about oil lamps? We've got to have something she can see if she comes back tonight."

"We have some flashlights. The big long ones."

"Good. They'll do. We'll leave the mainsail hoisted, and lash two of them to the shrouds so they'll shine on it. You can see an arrangement like that for miles."

"That's clever. I wouldn't have thought of it."

"It's an old trick in heavy traffic or poor visibility. Steamship captains trying to figure out what it is may call you things that'd raise blisters on a gun turret, but at least they won't run you down."

"I'm glad—" She stopped.

"What?"

"I was about to commit the incredible *gaucherie* of saying I was glad you'd come along. Let's just say that under other circumstances— May I relieve you at the pump now?"

"Are you sure you're not sleepy?"

"Yes."

"All right. You take over here, and I'll start bailing again."

He moved over to the hatch. Before he dropped the bucket in, he paused to look at an ugly mass of cloud along the horizon to the northeast. It looked like a nasty one, all right, but it was a long way off. He'd just have to keep an eye on it.

Saracen shuddered, protesting the engine vibration, and pitched with a long corkscrew motion as she continued to plow ahead. Here in the tiny compartment the air was stifling. Rae Ingram was conscious of thirst, and of the sour taste of vomit in her mouth. She sat on the bunk and stared unbelievingly at the barricaded door. She must be mad herself; Paradise couldn't have become this nightmare in the few short hours since sunrise, since this morning's dawn when she'd been alone with John on the immensity of the sea, when she'd swum nude beside the boat with that faint but shivery sensation of wickedness—and amusement, because it was a ridiculous way to act at thirty-five—when he'd used a whole quart of priceless fresh water to wash the salt out of her hair because, as he said, he loved her. Could you go from that to this in three hours? Numbly she looked down at her watch. It was 9:50. It had been a quarter of an hour since Warriner had restarted the engine and they'd got under way again.

She tried to force her mind to operate. She was apparently safe enough for the moment from any further assaults upon the door; as long as *Saracen* was under way, he had to be at the wheel. Also, he was apparently dangerous only when opposed. But that was unimportant. She still had to stop him. There was no way she could disable the engine now; she'd already grasped what that hammering was she'd heard in the after end of the main cabin. He'd nailed up the access to the engine compartment so she couldn't get in—at least without making enough noise to warn him. Mad or not, he would have taken some precaution, and that was simpler than trying to lock her in here. The door opened inward, and there was no bolt or hasp on the outside.

Then what? The only other place the engine could be stopped was at the control panel right in front of him in the cockpit. But wait, she thought suddenly. It had already been fifteen minutes since they'd started up again, and the other boat—what was it Warriner had called it, *Orpheus?*—had been almost hull down then. And from the sound of the engine it was still running at nearly full throttle. So merely stopping *Saracen* would do no good now, anyway. By this time they were out of sight over the horizon, and John would never know it. Then the whole problem was changed, and now it was even worse. Somehow she had to get control of the boat so she could take it back— Her thoughts broke off, and she sat up abruptly, feeling a chill along her spine.

Take it back? Back *where?*

She'd forgotten she had no idea at all which direction they'd been traveling since they'd left the other yacht. And with it lost somewhere over the horizon now, where all directions looked the same, trying to go back to it could be just as hopeless at ten miles as at a thousand. First of all and above everything else, she had to find out and keep track of their course. But how?

The answer occurred to her almost immediately. In one of the drawers under the bunks in the main cabin was a spare compass, a small one mounted on gimbals in a wooden box. She sprang up and began furiously hauling the sailbags from in front of the barricaded door. She dragged the cases of stores to one side, slid back the bolt, and peered out. The main cabin was empty.

It took only a minute. She hurried to the sink, softly pumped a cup of water, washed out her mouth, and drank, noting at the same time she'd been right about the access to the engine compartment. The panel was nailed shut. The compass was under the port bunk. Keeping an apprehensive eye on the hatch, she grabbed it out, snatched up a pencil and a pad of scratch paper from in back of the folding chart table, and slipped back inside the forward compartment.

She was about to close the door when another thought occurred to her. While she was able to get out into the other cabin, why not try the radio? If she did it carefully, there was a good chance Warriner wouldn't hear her. Of course! It was worth the risk.

He'd said the radio on the other boat was ruined by

water, but he'd also said he'd used it trying to call them. Which was the truth? It would take only a few minutes to find out. If it was still in working order, John would have turned it on, waiting; there was no doubt at all of that. Keyed up with excitement, she set the compass on the bunk with a pillow against it to keep it from rolling off, and slipped back out the door, closing it softly behind her.

The radio was mounted on bulkhead brackets above the after end of the starboard bunk, the transmitter and receiver in one unit. From there she was still invisible to Warriner at the wheel, and by facing toward the hatch she'd be able to see it darken even before his legs appeared if he started down. There was a loudspeaker, but a switch for cutting it out. She threw the switch to the off position, turned on the receiver, and set the bandswitch to 2638 kilocycles, one of the two intership bands.

Still nervously watching the hatch, she lifted the handset off its bracket. This actuated the switch starting the transmitter. The little rotary converter whirred softly; there was no chance Warriner could hear it above the noise of the engine. She put the handset to her ear and adjusted the gain of the receiver. The tubes had warmed up now. Static popped and hissed, but no one was calling. She reached over and turned the bandswitch to 2738 kilocycles. This was dead too, except for the static.

The transmitter was warmed up now. She pressed the handset button and adjusted the antenna tuning control for maximum indication on the meter. It was working beautifully.

"*Saracen* to *Orpheus*," she whispered into the microphone, though there was really no necessity to say anything; as soon as John heard the carrier come on he'd know who it was. There was nobody else out here. "This is the yacht *Saracen* calling *Orpheus*. Come in, please."

She released the transmit button and listened. Static crackled. She waited thirty seconds. Forty. There was no answer. She called again. There was still no response, no sound of a carrier coming on the air. If he was listening, it must be on the other band; maybe it was the only one *Or-*

pheus had. She threw the bandswitch and retuned the antenna control.

"*Saracen* to *Orpheus*, *Saracen* to *Orpheus*," she whispered. "This is the yacht *Saracen* calling *Orpheus*. Answer on either band. Come in, please."

She cut the transmitter and listened again, turning the bandswitch back and forth between the two channels. The only sound was the eternal crackling and hissing of static from far-off squalls pursuing their violent paths across the wastes of the southern hemisphere. She called twice more on each channel. There was no answer. She replaced the handset, turned off the receiver, and went back inside the forward cabin, wishing now she hadn't thought of the radio.

[9]

BUT SHE STILL HAD THE COMPASS. SHE PICKED IT UP FROM the bunk, removed the lid from the box, and looked about for a place to set it. It had to be oriented as nearly as possible in a plane with the vessel's fore-and-aft centerline, and it had to be secured so it couldn't move. The after bulkhead, she thought, to the right of the door and far enough away from it so it wouldn't be disturbed by moving the sailbags. She set it on the deck with the after side of the box flush with the bulkhead and cast about for something to hold it in place. Not cases of canned goods; cans were steel. One of the sailbags, of course; there was an extra one. She shoved it up against the forward side of the box. That would hold it.

She knelt beside it, studying the movements of the card. It was reading 227 degrees. Then 228 . . . 229 . . . 228 . . . 227 . . . 226 . . . 226 . . . 225 . . . 224 . . . 223 . . . 224, 225, 226 . . . 226 . . . 226 . . . At the end of two or three minutes it had swung no further than from 220 to 231 degrees, and most of the time had remained between 223 and 229. The course he was steering was probably 226 degrees. She glanced at her watch and wrote it down on the scratch pad.

10:14 AM   226 degrees   Est. speed 6 knots

That would do it, she thought. All that was necessary now was to keep watch on it to see if he changed. There was no certainty, she knew, that this reading of 226 degrees was anywhere near the actual course, the one he was steering in the cockpit; they might even differ by as much as 20 or 30 degrees. John had already taught her that much about the care and the mysterious natures of magnetic compasses. That one up there had been corrected by a professional compass-adjuster who'd inserted in the binnacle the bar magnets necessary to cancel out the errors induced by the vessel's own magnetism, mostly from the massive iron keel and the engine. This one wasn't adjusted, of course, and was in a different location besides, but it didn't matter as long as it didn't move out of the alignment it was in now. All she had to do, if she ever got control of the boat, was to put it on a general heading of 226 on this compass and then take the correct reading off that one in the cockpit. It wouldn't be easy, and it would take a lot of running back and forth to average out the error of several tries, but it could eventually be done within an accuracy necessary for the job of retracing their route from the other boat. Provided it wasn't too far . . .

For a few minutes she'd forgotten the rest of the problem in her satisfaction at being able to solve this minor part of it, but it all rushed back now and hit her like an icy sea. She sat down, weak-kneed, on one of the other sailbags and regarded end-to-end those two conditions she'd danced across separately and so lightly a moment before.

If she ever got control of the boat . . . Provided it wasn't too far . . .

How was she going to get control of it?

Trying to reason with him, she had already discovered,

was futile. Trying to overpower him was so manifestly absurd there was no point wasting time even thinking about it. There was the further fact, already demonstrated, that he regarded any interference with his flight—and probably opposition of any kind—as part of some terrifying conspiracy against his life, and while he was in the grip of this delusion he wouldn't hesitate to kill her. Five minutes later he would be sorry, and he'd probably cry over her body, but that wouldn't do her a great deal of good if she was already dead. Nor, more to the point, would it save John. So anything she tried from now on had to succeed the first time.

In the back of her mind, of course, there'd been the knowledge that in the end he had to go to sleep sometime. Then she would simply tie him up, turn the boat around, and go back to get John. But now, a little fearfully, she brought this comforting backlog out into the light and began to examine it more closely. In the first place, you couldn't tie a man up just because he was asleep; he'd wake up. So she'd have to hit him on the head with something. She knew nothing whatever about knocking people unconscious by hitting them on the head, in spite of the easy and apparently painless way it appeared to be accomplished all the time on television, and unless she was able to overcome her natural revulsion to such an act and did it brutally enough and in the right place he'd only wake up and choke her to death. And in the second place, how about that panel into the engine compartment? If he'd remembered to nail that up so she couldn't tamper with the engine again, he certainly wasn't going to go to sleep and leave himself unprotected. All he had to do was close the companion hatch and fasten it on the outside, and she'd be locked below.

But it was the third objection that finally wrecked it. He wasn't going to sleep—not in time to save John. Whatever horror he was fleeing from was still pursuing him down the dark corridors of the mind, and as long as the engine continued to run, he would. She knew no more about abnormal mental states than the average layman, but she was aware that a man in the grip of obsession or some pathological fear could be immune to fatigue for incredible lengths of time. He'd stay right there at the wheel until the engine died for lack of fuel.

How much gasoline did they have? *Saracen*'s cruising range on power was around two hundred miles. The tank had been full when they left Panama, but John ran the engine for short periods every day or so to charge the batteries and to keep the engine itself from succumbing to the saturated humidity of the tropics. Call it a total of ten hours in the nineteen days. At the moderate speed John drove the engine when he was using it, that would be forty-five or fifty miles. So at cruising speed they should have fuel for a hundred and fifty miles or about thirty hours. But Warriner was running the engine almost wide open, which would increase the fuel consumption tremendously. She wasn't sure how much, but John had said once that beyond a certain point increasing the speed one knot would almost double it. So call it fifteen to eighteen hours, at six knots. And from nine o'clock this morning . . . Sometime between midnight tonight and three o'clock tomorrow morning they would run out of fuel, ninety to a hundred and ten miles from that foundering hulk John was trapped on.

Then what?

The answer was short, inescapable, and merciless. She'd never find it again.

Assume Warriner *was* incautious enough to drop off to sleep in the cockpit without locking her below, and she was able to knock him out and tie him up—she'd have no fuel, of course, to go back with, so she'd have to sail back. In the interminable calms and fickle airs they'd been fighting for the past two weeks, that could take three or four days. But that wasn't the really deadly part of it, not by far. Sailing back, she just wouldn't find the place; she couldn't navigate well enough.

Steering a course under power was one thing; averaging out a course while you were beating all over the ocean on a dozen different headings at varying speeds for different lengths of time, and drifting helplessly at the mercy of uncertain currents for long periods of calm was something else entirely. The only way you could do it over any distance at all was with competent celestial navigation. John was teaching her, and she knew how to use the tables, but she was nowhere near accurate enough yet with the sextant. She could do it if she was trying to make a landfall on some headland visible thirty miles at sea, but if she missed the other yacht by more than four miles she'd never see it at all.

This was besides the fact that at the end of three or four days it wouldn't even be in the same place anyway. Even if it were too full of water to move under sail, currents would still act on it.

And it was sinking. She'd seen herself, from the way it lurched from side to side on the groundswell, there was lots of water in it, and the radio was dead.

Sometime around sunset this evening they would pass the point of no return. After that, they would have used up more than half the gasoline, and every ten minutes would be another mile that nothing would ever buy back—

Sunset. Suddenly, and with such piercing clarity it made her cry out, she saw him struggling in the water, alone on the emptiness of the sea, as the sun went down and the colors began to fade. She could see every line and angle of the face her finger tips had come to know so well, the sun-wrinkles at the corners of the eyes, and that horrible way she had cut his hair; the eyes themselves were open, the clear, cool gray eyes that could be ironic or amused but were far more often gentle, and there seemed to be no fear in them even now but only something she thought was sadness or regret. He made no sound. And there was no lifebelt. If you ever lost a boat, he'd said once, in a place where there was no chance of being picked up, you were better off without it.

She began to shake, all over and uncontrollably, and fell back on the pile of sailbags with the back of her left forearm pressed against her opened mouth while tears welled up in her eyes and overflowed. Why sunset? Why did she have to think of sunset? But she knew, remembering the moments of splendor and that shared enraptured silence when the world was only two people and a boat and a fragment of time poised between night and day. Would he be thinking of them? Would he have to? She was up then, throwing the sailbags behind her to clear the door. She slammed the cases of stores aside as if they were empty, and snatched up a marlinspike she somehow saw in her wildness lying among the coils of rope. Her hand was yanking at the bolt to open the door when some vestige of reason made itself heard at last and she was able to stop herself. She sagged against the bulkhead.

One chance was all she would get. She couldn't throw it away.

He was a young man, with a young man's reflexes. No matter how fast or unexpectedly she leaped into the cockpit she couldn't attack him that way and expect to accomplish anything but her own destruction. And with hers, John's. God, why did she have to be so helpless? There must be some way to stop him. There *had* to be.

It was then she remembered the shotgun.

Her mind slid away from it in revulsion. It edged back, reluctantly but compelled. She could see its dismembered pieces—two, she thought there were—wrapped in their separate strips of oiled fleece in one of the drawers under the starboard bunk. John had never assembled it since he'd brought it aboard, but he did check it from time to time to be sure it hadn't been attacked by rust. He was going to hunt something with it in Australia, or maybe it was New Zealand. In the same drawer were two boxes of its ammunition. . . .

It was sickening. It was impossible. Why was she even thinking about the thing? And there was no use trying to threaten him with it. You couldn't threaten a madman.

She looked down then and saw she still had the marlinspike in her hand. It was over a foot long, of heavy bright steel, gently tapering from one thick end to a point at the other—the classic weapon, she knew from the sea stories she'd read, of the bucko mates of nineteenth-century square-riggers driving their crews around the Horn. She'd never be able to hit him with it from in front, but suppose she could get behind him?

She might. His reactions were unpredictable, of course,

but there seemed a chance he wouldn't attack her out of hand if she came on deck, at least as long as she didn't appear to be trying to interfere with him. And he'd turned his back on her before. But that was before she'd tried to sabotage the engine, she thought; he'd be suspicious of her now. Well, she could look out the companion hatch and see how he reacted before she went too far.

There was another thing, too, she thought with growing excitement: once behind him, she could take a quick look into the binnacle and *see* what course he was steering. That would do away with all the trouble and possible inaccuracies of this other way.

The marlinspike would have to be well concealed, but still where it could be withdrawn swiftly and without catching on anything. She experimented. After pulling up the bottom of her blouse, she shoved it into the waistband of the Bermuda shorts and down the outside of her left thigh. But the shorts were a snug fit in this area, and it showed when she walked. She moved it around in front of the hip, where it angled down the hollow of her groin to the inside of the thigh. It had passed inside her nylon briefs, and the steel had a cold and alien feel against her skin. That was better as far as concealment was concerned, but she was aware now of the error of having it inside the shorts at all. When she withdrew it, she had it by the wrong end. The place for it was inside the blouse, which was looser anyway. With the heavy end caught under her arm and only the point inside the waistband, it lifted out easily and quickly and was held just right to swing. Conscious of the extreme shallowness of her breathing, she slid back the bolt and opened the door.

She crossed the after cabin, mounted the first step of the ladder, and peered cautiously out. Her head was still below the level of the deckhouse, but she could see him—or rather, she could see his head and the naked shoulders. He was seated behind the wheel, staring into the binnacle.

He still hadn't looked up, and she had no intention of venturing farther into his territory until he'd seen her and she could assess his reaction. From here she could still make it back to safety before he could get out from behind the wheel and catch her, but going too far would be like misjudging the length of chain by which some dangerous wild animal was secured. She waited, thinking of this and conscious of the incongruity or even the utter madness of the simile. Dangerous? This nice, well-mannered, unbelievably handsome boy who might have stepped right out of a mother's dream? That was the horror of it, she thought. Conscious evil or malicious intent you could at least communicate with, but Warriner was capable of destroying her with the pointlessness and the perfect innocence of a falling safe, and with its same imperviousness to argument.

He glanced up then and saw her. He smiled in evident pleasure and said something she couldn't hear above the noise of the engine. It might be a trick, of course, to entice her within range, but she had to risk it. She went up the ladder, trying to hold her arm as naturally as possible while it clamped the end of the marlinspike inside her blouse. The sea was still like glass, aside from the long undulations of the swell, and after the dimness below she was dazzled for a moment by the shimmering glow of sunlight reflected from it. She stepped out onto the narrow strip of deck along the starboard side of the cockpit, very scared now and pretending to look aft along their wake as though searching for the other boat. Slowly, she thought; stop a minute, and then another step or two, and don't try to smile; that would be too phony—

"No," he said. "Sit down there." He indicated the starboard cockpit seat and then added, "Where I can see you."

It was impossible to tell by his tone or manner whether he suspected her of something, but she hesitated only a second. She didn't have to go all the way back at once, and it would never do to argue with him. "Why?" she asked, but she sat down, some two or three feet forward of the binnacle and the wheel, with her left arm falling naturally at her side.

"Because your face fascinates me," he said, tilting his head slightly to the left and leaning over the wheel to view it better. "You have no idea what a study it would have made the way you were looking up and out at me like some hesitant naiad from a grotto—no. Naiads were Greek. You're Scandinavian."

"Partly," she managed to say. She didn't even know whether he'd meant it as a question or not.

"Oh, definitely Scandinavian. Under your clothes you're probably as blond as snow." He smiled, as though to reassure her that at their level of sophistication there was nothing tendentious in this discussion of her private blondness. "But it was your face we were talking about, the magnificent bone structure. Do you know you'll still be a beautiful woman when you're eighty? I'm speaking as a professional. I'm a painter, and painters always approach a face from the other side, to see what's holding it up. Those high cheekbones and the tilted eyes are racial, of course; people say Slavic, or Tartar, or a half-dozen other things, but to me they're always Scandinavian. If they came out of western or central Asia it must have been along the Arctic Circle. . . ."

He was still too far away to hit, even if he should happen to turn his head. For a moment she saw the whole scene with a sort of wondering horror—a civilized woman of the twentieth century, sitting here with a marlinspike of the Cape Stiff bully-boys secreted against her flesh between her nylon panties and her bra, listening while this handsome boy who was murdering her husband as surely as if he'd used a gun discussed with such charm and evident admiration the structure of her face. How much more of it could she stand? The point of no return was sunset, and if she was still alive then she'd be as mad as he was.

It wasn't that she couldn't do anything, she thought, trying to isolate or identify the ultimate nightmare quality of it; she wasn't tied, or locked up, or even openly threatened, and there was nothing to stop her now from leaping across that narrow space with the marlinspike aswing—nothing except that it might fail, and one chance was all she was going to get. It always came back to that. She had a life expectancy of just one more unsuccessful attempt to stop him, and then John would drown.

Then was she already becoming paralyzed with indecision, like the boy with only one dime in a candy store, unable to make up his mind until the store had already closed and he was out on the sidewalk? She didn't know, but she could see it coming. The stakes were too high, the pressure too brutal. Nobody was equipped to hold entirely in his hands the life of the person he loved above everything else on earth—no, not even in his hands, but poised like an egg on the back of one of them as though for an obstacle race in some macabre party game. Not even professionals, she thought; the surgeon called in another surgeon when the life of his own child was at stake.

[10]

BUT WHEN HE WAS QUIET LIKE THIS—IF NOT RATIONAL, AT least for the moment not in the seizure of that torment or terror—why in God's name couldn't she get through to him? It was obvious at a glance what kind of boy he was, and the way he'd been brought up; he'd open doors for you, give you his seat on a bus, or bring you a drink at a cocktail party. And while she suspected there might not be any great strength in him, there was no doubt he was educated, civilized, and probably incapable of deliberate evil or pointless cruelty until this thing, whatever it was, had happened to him. Then why wasn't she able to reach in past the snarled wire-ends of his broken lines of communication and make contact with him, get him to realize what he was doing?

Maybe she hadn't tried hard enough. Or she'd tried in the wrong way; she'd been half hysterical herself, and she'd screamed at him. And then she'd talked down to him, as though it were a recognized fact between them there was something wrong with his mind. Of course, she'd known the error of this the moment it was done, but it was too late to correct.

Anyway, try once more, she thought, and with a better approach; see if you can't establish some kind of contact before even bringing up the subject of going back. Get him to talk about himself? No-o. She hated to throw out the oldest weapon in the arsenal, but there she'd be flirting with the very danger she had to avoid, any reminder of the horror he was fleeing. The past, maybe, but stay away from the voyage; whatever it was happened at sea. Talk about painting, even if you don't know much about it, talk about yourself. That was it, she thought; if she could establish an identity he could recognize, first merely as a woman who was friendly and sympathetic, and then as one he could help in some way, she might penetrate the insularity of breakdown and get through, at least temporarily, to the old behavior patterns. God, if she could only get him to pick up the phone.

". . . it's an overworked word," he was saying, "but definitely valid here. I know I could feel it."

She came back with a start. Was he still talking about her face? "I'm sorry," she said, "but I missed that. What was it?"

"Empathy," he replied. "Sometimes you meet people you're in full conversation with before a word has ever been said. It was that way when I first saw you. Oh, I don't mean the sex thing—though God knows you have plenty of that." Again his smile included her among the mature and the intelligent. He glanced into the compass and then back at her, leaning over the wheel. "I knew we'd like each other. I knew I could talk to you, and neither of us would need an interpreter. But I don't even know your first name yet."

"It's Rae," she said. It was starting out beautifully; he was doing it himself. There were cigarettes and a lighter in the right-hand pocket of the Bermuda shorts. She took them out and tried to light one. In the six-knot breeze of their passage, it didn't take too much acting ability to fail three times in succession.

"Here, let me," he offered.

He lit the cigarette for her and passed it back, and lit one for himself. Good, she thought; one conditioned response might lead to another, and then another. . . . Then it occurred to her she could be oversimplifying just a little the labyrinthine complexities of modern psychiatry; if doctors spent lifetimes trying to find out why a mind went off the rails and how to get it back, there seemed a chance it wasn't quite that easy. But at least she was doing something. *Saracen* heaved up and swayed, quartering the long groundswell. Sunlight shattered into golden points of fire in his hair, and the fine gray eyes were alight with interest as they continued to search her face. She tried not to remember the way they'd looked when he was strangling her.

"Thank you, Hughie," she said simply. Don't overdo it; don't gush.

"Je vous en prie, madame."

"I'm sorry, I don't speak French." She was about to add that John was teaching her Spanish, but didn't. Probably it was best to keep John out of it until she had some kind of bridge across the gap.

"I detect just a trace of Southern accent, I think. From where?"

"Texas," she replied.

"Oil?"

She shook her head. "Every area has its slum dwellers. There are Texans who don't own oil wells."

"See, I knew we'd like each other." Then he added, "I'm from Mississippi. Or was originally." He explained briefly he'd gone to school in Switzerland and spent most of his life in Europe.

"Are your parents still there?" she asked.

"No," he said. "My mother's dead. She died six years ago."

"I'm sorry. But your father is still living?"

The change in him was startling, attuned as she was to every nuance of his expression. "No!" he said loudly. "I mean—I don't know!" Agitation was evident in his eyes, and she could sense his desperate groping through the mists in back of them. Then he appeared to regain control. "I mean, I haven't seen him for years. He still lives in Mississippi, and we never write to each other."

She breathed softly. That had been close. It was obvious she'd made a mistake, but she couldn't understand where or how. Surely his father hadn't been on the boat. Pretend you didn't see it, she told herself, and change the subject, fast.

But he had already fully recovered, as though it had never happened. He smiled at her and said, "Never mind me; you still haven't told me anything about yourself. Except that you're from Texas, which you'll admit yourself is trite. When they get to the moon, they'll find out there's not only a Texan there, but he's already bought it, air-conditioned it, and organized a local chapter of the John Birch Society. *I* could tell you more than that about yourself, just for a start. The chances are you weren't an only child; you had a very good orthodontist when you were young, or ancestors with exceptional teeth; you're warm-hearted, and you have a great deal of sympathy and understanding, but you're impulsive; and status probably means little or nothing to you. All surface, of course, and some guesswork. So you take it. Tell me what the leopard was looking for on the slopes of Kilimanjaro." His gesture included all the vast and empty Pacific. "Just a parking place, or did he hear music?"

And the leopard was dead, she thought. But more immediately, that lightning reversal of mood was ominous; even when he was like this, he was further from reality than she'd believed. Well, you still had to try.

"He heard music," she said. "Perhaps not very good music, and maybe even sentimental, or trite. But he also saw something up there."

"What?" he asked. "Samarkand? A trail disappearing into the mist? Not the edge of a map, because maps don't have edges any more. The just say continued on E-12."

"No," she said. "What he saw was simply another leopard listening to the same thing. A rather handsome leopard in a furry and beat-up sort of way, with the same odd taste for Mickey Mouse music and listening to it in strange places. It was like this."

She didn't like doing it; revealing herself this way to a stranger was too much like filling out a Kinsey questionnaire or undressing in public, but, weighed against any possible chance of success, the cost was small. She took a puff on her cigarette and wondered where to begin. Anywhere, she thought, just so you can make him see you.

"One night about a year ago a man came to the hotel where I was registered in Miami, Florida. He was a curt, rather hard-bitten sort of man with too much arrogance and a slight limp, and I didn't think I liked him. And apparently it was mutual; he didn't seem to think too highly of me. I did believe he was honest, though, which was important in the particular circumstances. And the reason I thought he was honest was that anybody that disagreeable and that indifferent to the impression he made on other people almost had to be.

"The reason for our being there—for my being in Miami at all, and for his being in my hotel room—was a yacht, a big two-masted schooner named *Dragoon*. It was mine—or had been. It also had quite a bit to do with the lack of friendliness in the meeting. In the first place, there was probably a sensed difference of attitude as to what a sailing yacht really was. To me it was just a piece of property, like a parcel of land or a stock certificate, that I happened to own, mostly by accident, and which I'd been aboard only once in the two years I had owned it. To him a boat—a good one—represented something else. But besides this, and much more important, was the fact *Dragoon* had just been stolen, and he was suspected by police of having helped to steal it. They'd picked him up and questioned him, and then released him because they didn't have any actual proof, not enough to hold him. I gathered from the police they'd had a difficult time with him; he wasn't a man who took kindly to being called a thief.

"But first maybe I'd better explain how I happened to own a two-masted sailing yacht in the first place, since I cared nothing at all about boats then. I was a widow, and not even a wealthy one—just a lonely one. I'd been married for a long time and very happily to a quiet and gentle man who was also one of the coldest-nerved and most fantastic gamblers I've ever known. His name was Chris Osborne, and I suppose you'd say he was in the real-estate business, though real-estate speculation would be more like it. By the time he was forty-five he'd already made and lost several fortunes. I'd been his secretary before we were married, but even with that edge I don't think I was ever sure at any given moment whether we were very well off or in debt. Not that it mattered a great deal. Without any children—" She couldn't bring herself to mention the son who'd died. To a boy as young as Warriner it would mean very little anyway, and there had to be a limit somewhere to the coin you were willing to spend to get his attention. "Without any children to leave it to, I could never see any point in piling up money you didn't need. We were happy, which was the thing that counted. Except that of course he was away a lot. I wasn't much good at the social routine, because I'd worked most of my life, and women from better backgrounds and expensive schools could always make me feel awkward and put me on the defensive—I mean the ones who wanted to. So I had a business of my own, just for something to do when he was away, a small sports-car agency. But none of that's important.

"Chris was killed three years ago. He'd gone out to Lubbock to look at a cattle ranch he was interested in, and the plane he was flying went out of control in a thunderstorm and crashed. I won't burden you with what it's like becoming a widow just by picking up the telephone, but it's one of those things you get through some way, then and afterward. It took nearly two years to straighten out his business affairs. He was overextended again and pretty thinly financed on several deals he was working on, and there was a tax case pending with the Internal Revenue Service. There wasn't a great deal left in the end, but I worked it out as well as I could. And it was something to do.

"But to get on to *Dragoon*. Chris didn't care anything about boats either; he'd simply taken it in as part payment on some deal in Florida real estate, intending to sell it later. Then he was killed, and during the two years it took to get the estate settled and pay off the tax bill it lay at anchor in Key West with a watchman living aboard. Then, just as I started advertising it for sale, it was stolen. Some men got the old watchman drunk ashore and took it out of the harbor one night. The police called me in Houston, and I flew down there. They had only two leads to work on. One was that *Dragoon*'s dinghy had been picked up at sea by a fishing boat southeast of Miami near the Great Bahama Bank. The other was a suspect.

"It seemed a man had been aboard the yacht just a few days before, looking it over, and told the watchman he was interested in it. The watchman remembered his name, and the police picked him up at the hotel where he was staying in Miami and questioned him. They'd found out who he was, and were satisfied with his references—he'd been a charter yacht captain in the Bahamas for a long time, and had operated a shipyard in San Juan, Puerto Rico, until he'd got badly burned in an explosion and fire that destroyed most of it—but they weren't satisfied with his story as to why he'd been interested in *Dragoon*.

"He said he'd been hired to take a look at it by a businessman staying at one of the big Miami Beach hotels, the president of some pharmaceutical firm, who wanted to buy a boat for company entertaining and asked him for a professional opinion of *Dragoon* before making me an offer subject to final survey. But when the police checked, the businessman turned out to be a phony. There was no such company, and the man himself had checked out of the hotel the same night *Dragoon* was stolen. So it was obvious he was one of the thieves. The only thing the police still weren't sure of was whether this man was also one of the thieves or just another victim.

"So that's when he came to see me at the hotel, just after he'd been questioned by the police, this hard-bitten and disagreeable man with the limp. His name was John Ingram, he said, and he was going to help me find my boat. I offered to pay him and was curtly brushed off. There would be no charge, he said. I was glad to have his help, but I still wasn't any fonder of him. I could be stubborn too, and I didn't like having favors tossed at me in that manner.

"But at the same time I began to have a very funny feeling about it. We'd find the boat. We'd find it if he had to sift the Atlantic Ocean with a tea-strainer. Maybe the thieves had made a mistake stealing it in the first place, but their really sad mistake was ever getting this man involved in it.

"He had an idea it was in trouble, probably out there somewhere near where the dinghy had been found, so we chartered a seaplane in Nassau to search the area from the air, and we finally located it aground on a sandbar on the edge of the Great Bahama Bank, about a hundred and fifty miles southeast of Miami. The pilot landed us, with a rubber raft, and we went aboard. Two of the men who'd stolen it were still on it. They'd been trying to run a cargo of guns to one of the Central American countries, when they'd run up onto the Bank from poor navigation.

"John got the boat away from them, refloated it—without a towboat—threaded it through all those shoals and sandbars into deep water again, and sailed it back to Miami. I watched him do it; otherwise I probably wouldn't have believed it. But that isn't what I started out to tell you, not just a story of watching an indomitable man do the impossible against a background I didn't even know existed, nor even the fact that I got my boat back. Long before we reached Florida I didn't care whether we ever did, and *Dragoon* had ceased to be important at all. I was just terrified he was going to sail it into Miami, tie it up, step off onto the dock, and say, 'Now, Mrs. Osborne, there's your goddamned boat,' and turn around and walk away without even looking back. And if he did I knew I couldn't stand it. It was as simple as that.

"I realize you can't even become acquainted with somebody in five days, let alone fall in love with him. But it happened. Maybe it was the slow-motion effect of time and that increased sensitivity to everything you have in an unusual situation. Maybe it was from being with him every minute there in his own element, this world that was so strange and so utterly fascinating to me, as if I were actually seeing him for the first time. As I was. He wasn't an arrogant and disagreeable man at all, but just a very proud one who felt he'd been made a fool of. And a very lonely one. He tried to hide it under all that armor of self-sufficiency, the way he fought the limp from those burns, but it was as clear to me as if he'd been carrying a sign.

"The same thing was happening to him, and he didn't walk away when we got to Miami, but naturally it wasn't as hasty and impulsive as all that, not with either of us. It took some time to clear myself of the suspicion of being some wealthy and socially prominent man-eater who was trying to buy him for a pet, and to convince him that I didn't have any more money than he did. Then he pointed out that I'd seen him only in his own environment, and he'd look entirely different in mine—that is, living and working ashore. That wasn't true, of course, but I knew he would be unhappy. But it was a dead issue anyway; there was nothing in my old life I wanted to go back to. I was as in love with this exciting new world of his just as much as he was, and I had a simpler approach to the subject of environment anyway. Mine was any place that included him. But then I warned you this was sentimental and probably corny.

"We were married six months later, after I'd wound up all the loose ends in Houston and sold everything I didn't want to be burdened with any more. I sold *Dragoon,* which was too big for two people to handle, and we bought *Saracen.* Some day we expect we may go into the charter business in the Bahamas or West Indies, but that's in the future. Now we're on our honeymoon. We're on our way to Tahiti. We realize it has jet runways now, but there are places beyond that don't. We don't know how long the cruise will last nor how far we'll go. Maybe we'll simply go broke. We don't really care. I suppose you could call it a juvenile dream, or flight from responsibility, or refusal to accept the challenge, but everybody doesn't have to listen to the same drum. I like ours. I fell in love with it the first time I heard it, one night on a grounded schooner on the Great Bahama Bank, when I discovered what *he* was listening to and that I was in love with him. I've heard it ever since. I heard it this morning at dawn, becalmed a thousand miles from land, when he woke me winding a chronometer, and in a hundred other places and times and different kinds of weather, and always with him. If it ever stopped, or anything happened to him, I don't think I'd want to go on living." She paused and took a deep breath to steady the shaky feeling inside her. If she hadn't reached him, she never would.

"Now, Hughie," she went on quietly, "don't you think it's time we went back?"

His eyes had been on her face throughout with that same look of interest. Now he appeared to be caught off guard by this abrupt change of subject.

"Back?" he asked politely.

"Yes. To get John."

"You mean back *there?*"

"Yes. We have to, Hughie. You realize that as well as I do—"

He shook his head. "Of course we can't go back."

She held on tightly. Don't scream at him. Don't lose your head. Some of it *must* have got through. "Hughie, please—" But how in God's name could you keep repeating the obvious *without* the appearance of talking down, of explaining something to an idiot? How did you keep it on an intelligent level after you'd said it a dozen times? There simply wasn't any way. "We have to go back now, Hughie. Now, before it's too late."

"No," he said with a little shrug of annoyance. She could see him beginning to go away, as though she had disappointed him again with this revelation of selfishness in her character.

"Hughie, he's my husband. I love him. Do you think I could go off and leave him on a sinking boat, to drown? You can't, either; you know you can't. You're not capable of a thing like that. How could you justify it? You couldn't live with yourself—"

"Do you always have to ruin everything by becoming hysterical? He won't drown."

"But that boat is sinking!"

"Why do you keep saying that?"

"You said it was. You told us yourself."

"I did?" It was obvious he didn't believe it. He glanced into the binnacle, dismissing the whole thing as of no importance. "I don't know why I would have said a thing like that."

"Well, if it's not sinking, why did you abandon it and come on here?"

"Why?" He looked up sharply. "Because they're trying to kill me."

She knew she was skirting the precipice now, but there was no way to avoid it. You couldn't plead with him to go back without running into his reasons for not going. "Who's trying to kill you?"

"Both of them." His expression changed then, becoming one of triumphant slyness. "But I fooled them. They'll never get me now, even with your husband helping them."

There it was, she thought. They had come full circle and were back facing each other across the unbridgeable chasm. But at least he hadn't become violent, and if she could stay here and go on talking maybe eventually she could get behind him. The marlinspike was cold and frightening against her flesh.

"Hughie," she said soothingly, "nobody wants to kill you—"

"What?"

"I said nobody wants to hurt you."

The craftiness in his eyes became more pronounced. "You mean I just imagined it?"

She saw the trap and tried to avoid it. "No, I mean it must be a mistake, a misunderstanding of some kind—"

"No! I know what you meant. You think there's something wrong with me, don't you?"

"Of course I don't, Hughie."

"Oh, yes, you do. You're just the same as they were. First your husband, and now you! Poor Hughie's subject to hallucinations!" His voice slipped up into falsetto, apparently in imitation of someone, and was charged with an indescribable bitterness. "You just imagined it, Hughie, dear. Of course you did, darling."

"Hughie! Stop that!" She tried to sound stern and forceful. Maybe she could shock him out of it.

His hands tightened on the wheel, and his eyes were on her with the beginnings of wildness in them. "And I thought I could trust you! I thought you were like Estelle!"

She could only stare in terror then. The name itself seemed to do something to him, to goad him beyond reason. Tendons stood out in his throat, and muscles writhed along his arms and shoulders as he tried to pull the wheel loose, or shake it. He cried out as though something were tearing inside him, and began to shout, leaning toward her across the wheel. She could feel the drops of spittle on her arm.

"*They murdered her!* They tried to kill us both! And you want to take me back there, don't you, so they can finish the job? Oh, I know what you're trying to do!" He half rose from the seat, as if to come out from behind the wheel.

Trying to stop him with the marlinspike would be suicide. She'd only hit him on an upraised arm, and then he'd take it away from her. If she ran, it would almost certainly trigger pursuit, and he could catch her before she could make it to the forward cabin. She did the only thing that was left. She sat still, forcing herself not even to draw back from him. For a second that seemed to go on forever it hung there, and then he dropped back to the seat again.

"*They* did it!" he shrieked. "They did it!" He was staring straight in front of him, and she sensed that he had forgotten her. His lips continued to move, but he made no further sound, and a muscle kicked spasmodically under one eye.

She never knew how afterward, but she forced herself to remain seated for another thirty seconds. Then she stood up slowly and with exaggerated casualness, on legs that trembled and had to be locked at the knees to support her. He paid no attention. She stepped back into the hatchway and started down, still clasping the marlinspike under her arm. At the bottom her legs quit on her at last, but she made it to one of the bunks before she collapsed. She turned then and looked back at the hatch. Sunlight fell into it unobstructed, sweeping back and forth across the ladder treads as *Saracen* rolled. The clatter of the engine went on, and above it she could either hear or feel the pounding of her heart.

It was the starboard bunk she was on—her own, where John came to her when they made love. Above it was the radiotelephone that was powerless to reach him, its very silence a cry for help. And under it in one of the drawers was the shotgun. She had remembered it too easily this time. Her mind slipped away from it with the same revulsion, but she could still see it. She pushed herself off the bunk and ran on into the forward cabin and bolted the door.

It was 11:10 a.m. She raised her eyes from the watch and swept them around the tiny V-shaped compartment that was no longer a sanctuary or a haven but a corner. It even looked like one.

[11]

THERE WERE TWO CHOICES, AND SHE HAD SEVEN HOURS IN which to make up her mind. But both choices were impossible, and nobody could endure this for seven hours.

What happened then?

She could foresee the answer, but she went over it again, just to be sure. Her mind was operating quite coldly at the moment, and she was calm; she was stronger than she'd thought. But then this was only the beginning, and the show hadn't even started yet. She knew what was coming.

She could kill Warriner with the shotgun, or she could go off and leave John to drown. Since neither of these was even conceivable, she had the third, which wasn't an alternative choice but merely a statement of fact or at least of probable truth. Nobody could endure this for seven hours. Her nerves would crack. Sometime between now and sunset her whole nervous system would go up in a puff of smoke like a short-circuited pinball machine; bells would ring, lights would flash, and she'd wind up lying on the bunk staring blankly at nothing while she picked at the fuzz on the blankets. In which case, alternative number two would win by default, and John would drown anyway.

Was that all?

No. There was still one other possibility. At the moment her nerves snapped she might run out and attack Warriner with the marlinspike or with her bare hands. The result of that was foregone.

Then she had to kill Warriner, and she had to do it before just thinking of it drove her out of her mind.

No. She sat down on one of the sailbags with her hands pressed against her temples. Nothing in life could ever be reduced to as simple terms as that. There had to be some other way out of the corner.

Well, where was it? Try them all again.

Hit him with something? He was suspicious of her now, and she couldn't get behind him. And again you ran into the same old limiting factor; you'd get only one blow, and if that didn't work you were dead, and so was John.

Try once more to reason with him? After what had just happened? You could carry on long conversations with him on any subject in the world, except one. At the mere mention of going back, he retreated into his madness and pulled up the bridge.

Well, maybe John wouldn't drown; maybe *Orpheus* wasn't sinking. That there was no way of proving definitely, one way or the other, but she had the evidence of her own eyes that there was water in the boat, lots of water. And why didn't the radio work? Then she thought of something else. The engine didn't work either, or John would have followed them. So everything below was flooded. Even if it weren't in danger of sinking within the next few hours, John would never make port in it. Nobody could pump continuously for twenty days or more. Warriner said there were others aboard, but they hadn't been on deck, and they would have been. So either they didn't exist except in his madness, or they were hurt or already dead.

But at least she could try the radio again. She slid back the bolt and went out, carrying the marlinspike. If he started down the ladder she could throw it at his legs to be sure of getting back in time. She called and listened alternately on both the intership frequencies. There was no answer, no sound except the eternal crackling of the static. At the end of twenty minutes she knew she no longer had any hope of one, that she was only putting off the thing she had to face. She switched it off and went back. Very carefully and precisely she noted the heading on the compass and wrote it down on the scratch pad along with the time.

11:40 AM   226 degrees

It looked neat and businesslike. And there was the illusion she was doing something.

They hit her then from opposite sides, or rather she ran headlong into the second while she was recoiling from the first. The first, of course, was John. He was in the water, drowning, as the sun went down. She leaned forward with her face pressed against the scratch pad on her knees, her eyes tightly closed and then opened again because it was more clearly seen and more terrible with them closed. Then it was gone, as if an automatic projector were changing slides, and she saw the thing that would be there in the cockpit when the shotgun had done its work.

She'd never in her life shot anything with a gun of any kind, but her father and two older brothers had been hunters of quail, and inevitably she had seen a few examples of the mess that resulted when a bird was shot too close under the gun. She had no illusions as to what would be up there. She swallowed, fighting the nausea pushing up into her throat.

Seven hours?

Maybe she could merely frighten him with the gun, point it at him the way they did on television, and say, "All right, Hughie, turn around and go back." This, she knew in her heart, was idiocy comparable to that other cliché of the private eyes and western marshals, the immaculate and neatly packaged death by gunshot wound that never hurt, either the shooter or the shot, but she gathered it to her for a moment in the desperation of her need for some other way out of the corner. Granted there didn't seem to be much likelihood of scaring a man who was already insane from fear, you could at least examine it and try to figure out what would happen.

You had to assume two things, she thought. The first was that Hughie was capable of evaluating two different fears and making a conscious choice of the lesser. Could he? Probably, at least part of the time, but at any specific moment it would be as unpredictable as tossing a coin. The second was that a quaking matron with a gun would be more fearsome than the irrational horror that had already taken possession of his mind. No. Certainly not. The things in the darkness beyond the firelight were always more terrible than the ones that you could see. He'd either pay no attention to the gun at all, or at the mere mention of going back he'd go berserk and charge straight at her.

But it was still worth trying, wasn't it? Even if there was only one chance in a thousand she could bluff him into going back and could control him all the way there without actually having to shoot, at least there would be that one. No. She saw the stupidity of it. Trying to bluff a man she couldn't bluff, with a gun she hoped she wouldn't have to use, was nothing short of suicide. In that second when she was still hysterically voicing threats and praying he would stop before she had to shoot, it would be too late to shoot, even if she could, and he'd have the gun away from her and he'd kill her. If she took it up that ladder at all and committed herself, it had to be with the hundred-percent certainty she was prepared to use it. And that she didn't have.

Why not? It was Warriner, wasn't it, who'd backed her into this corner from which there was no other exit?

Legally there was no question of her right to do so. There would be a hearing, somewhere and sometime, at which she would have to testify as to the circumstances, but that was all. She wouldn't be charged with anything, and nobody would attach any blame to her. Then it was simply because of all those nights she'd wake up screaming, and the fact that until the day she died her mind would never emerge completely from the shadow of that unanswered question: could there have been some other way?

So in the end it boiled down to a simple act of purchase, didn't it? If she had no illusions about the price or about the fact she would have to pay it, the terms were clear and understood. For John's life she gave up her peace of mind for the rest of her own. Why not? People gave up their lives themselves for others, didn't they? This was the opposite of heroic, and the act itself was abhorrent, but the same love was involved, the same willingness to pay.

She realized then there was no sense to any of these arguments. You couldn't rationalize killing a man with a shotgun, and you didn't arrive at the deed by any process of thought, of weighing the advantages and disadvantages. If you did it at all, it was after you'd quit thinking, in desperation, when nothing else was left.

And, anyway, she probably couldn't even assemble the gun. John had never done it since it had been aboard, and it had been nearly twenty years since she'd seen her father do it. And it could be a different kind, or a later model. Guns must change over the years, the way cars did, didn't they? Of course they did.

But there were only two pieces.

No, it was just her impression there were only two pieces. There might be more. She'd never counted them, had she?

Well, if she found out she couldn't assemble it, that would settle it, and the torture would stop.

Then, without even knowing how she'd got there, she was kneeling beside the bunk in the after cabin, pulling out the drawer. There were only two rolls of the fleece, one long one and another shorter and bulkier. She ran back into the forward cabin with them and bolted the door. She put them on the bunk and begun untying the cords that bound them.

There were three pieces.

The long roll contained only the barrels, the twin dark

tubes fixed side by side, but the other held two pieces. One was the part that went against your shoulder—the stock, she thought it was called—with the lever for breaking it open to put in the shells, and the trigger guard and the triggers. The other piece was a hand-grip sort of thing she seemed to remember went under the barrels just in front of the stock. It was mostly of wood, rounded on the sides and bottom, tapering at one end and fitted with a concave piece of steel at the other. She had no idea how it was supposed to be attached to the barrels.

The barrels themselves had a projection at one end, on the bottom, that must fit into something in the metal part at the front end of the stock. She took them in one hand and the stock in the other and began trying to match them. Yes, there it was. They went together, and formed a hinge. She swung the barrels up, and they locked in place.

But there was still the third part.

And it was obvious it was the wrong piece for this kind of gun, or that something was missing. It was supposed to go under the barrels, right there, and there was nothing to hold it. The concave end must go against the rounded metal and there at the front of the stock. And you could see it didn't even fit; it still stuck out at a slight angle. Well, John must have ordered another one to be shipped to them in Papeete. And since the gun couldn't be assembled without the right piece— There was a little click, and she gasped. The fore end had snapped up into place against the spring tension that held it there.

She stared at it in horror. It was a complete shotgun. It was all there, and it was assembled.

For the third time in ten minutes Lillian Warriner saw Ingram glance off to the northeast where the squall flickered and rumbled along the rim of the world. She could see no appreciable difference in the squall itself. It was still the same swollen mass of purple, shot through with the fitful play of lightning and trailing its skirts of rain, seemingly no larger or nearer than it had been a quarter of an hour ago—but it was Ingram himself she was watching. She judged by the simple fact that he kept looking at it that he was worried about it, though he said nothing. He continued to bail, the gray eyes expressionless.

Well, it wasn't likely he'd be running in circles and wringing his hands. And there was nothing they could do about the squall anyway, except get the sail off, and probably he'd send her to wake Bellew. No doubt there was some quixotic male convention against allowing the porcine bastard to drown in his sleep.

She liked Ingram and was conscious of increasing admiration for him, though this of course only added to the burden of her guilt, while at the same time evoking a mild sort of wonder at her willingness to credit her appraisal of anybody any more after having been so conspicuously wrong about Bellew. No, it wasn't so much that she'd been wrong as that she'd simply had no way of knowing how small even a large yacht could become after a few days at sea. Human beings confined in too small an area were apparently subject to the same laws regarding molecular friction and the generation of heat as gases under compression.

So now not only had they managed to blow themselves up, but the spreading shock wave of disaster had engulfed two other people whose only crime had been the fact they were in the same part of the ocean. The guilt was still hers, and she accepted it, though it seemed a terrible price to pay for the pursuit of an impossible dream, a few minutes of arrant and unforgivable bitchiness, and an accident. There were beckoning avenues of escape: the accident couldn't have been her fault because she'd been asleep at the time, and she'd been goaded into the bitchiness, but these were sleazy evasions and technicalities for which she had nothing but contempt. They were the type of thing that Hughie— She stopped.

Well, it was true, wasn't it? And therein, unfortunately, lay her guilt, the real responsibility from which there would never be any escape—the pursuit of the impossible dream, while she knew it was impossible. She'd known it would never work, that temperamentally she was wrong for him and she'd demand too much of him, but she'd managed to ignore the warnings of her mind.

If only, she thought now in her own contained and private agony, she'd left him alone. She was worse than any of them; she'd utterly destroyed him. Because she did love him. She wondered what crimes the human race could have found to commit without those great ennobling causes like freedom, religion, and love.

She glanced up. Ingram had stopped bailing and was preparing to lower the mainsail. She looked out toward the squall still making up in the northeast. "Is it coming nearer?"

"I can't tell yet what it's going to do," he replied. "But there's no use letting the sails slat any longer."

"Do you want me to help?"

"No. Better keep pumping. Or just rest for a few minutes."

She was conscious of numbness in her arms and shoulders, but she shook her head. "No. I'm all right." She bent to the pump again.

If only she'd left him alone. . . .

The main and mizzen were tightly furled. Ingram finished lashing the genoa rolled up along the lifeline and looked at his watch. It was 3:50 p.m. The sun, though lower in the west, still beat on them with sullen weight in the sticky and unmoving air that felt as if you were trying to breathe in a vacuum. The day was a squall-breeder if he'd ever seen one. There was no sound except water going overboard from the pump and those other and inexorably increasing tons of it sloshing back and forth inside the hull as *Orpheus* lurched over on the swell. The whole northeast sky was black now, but then squalls always looked worse when they were opposite the sun. There was still a chance it would pass to the northward of them, and he didn't want to call Bellew. Not yet. Let him get all the sleep he could. There was a long night ahead of them—if they were still afloat.

He was conscious now of his own tiredness and of the fact he had eaten nothing since breakfast. But he wasn't hungry; it was too hot to eat, even if there was anything aboard not ruined by the water. He picked up the binoculars and climbed atop the deckhouse. Very slowly and carefully he searched the horizon all across the southwest, finding nothing but emptiness. When he lowered the glasses he saw Mrs. Warriner's eyes on him. He shook his head. She nodded, her face as expressionless as his own, and went on pumping.

He stepped back to the ventilating hatch and looked down at the water washing back and forth in the after cabin. It was worse, he thought; even with one of them pumping and one bailing, they were barely keeping up with it. He started to drop the bucket in but turned and glanced back at Mrs. Warriner. She was on the verge of collapse. The hell with it. There was no use letting her kill herself. He tossed the bucket on the deck, then went over and picked up her cigarettes and lighter from the deckhouse.

"Here," he said. He set one of the cigarettes between her teeth and flicked the lighter. "Let me take it for a while."

She surrendered the pump reluctantly. "But how about yourself? You haven't had any rest at all. And won't it gain?"

"It'll just have to gain. You're not going to help things by keeling over. And while you're resting, you could finish telling me what happened—that is, if you feel up to it."

She sat down on the deck, facing him. "It's not the pleasantest thing in the world to tell, but since we did this to you, I'd say you had every right to know *how* we did it." She took a puff on the cigarette and went on. "To understand why he thinks we tried to murder him, you need a little background and a thumbnail sketch of the characters involved. Hughie, as I've told you, was an oversheltered boy who never had a chance to grow up; Mrs. Bellew was a rather plain, very gentle woman with an infinite amount of compassion; Bellew, of course, is a pig; and I'm an arrogant and insufferable bitch."

Ingram paused in his pumping. "Do you have to do that?"

She wondered herself. She'd always held a dim view of the therapeutic value of catharsis or confession and regarded all breast-beating and cries of *mea culpa* as being more vulgar exhibitionism than anything else. If you'd bought it, you lived with it as well as you could and with a little fuss as possible. But on the other hand, if you'd wronged another human being, you at least owed him an explanation.

"You wanted to understand, didn't you?" she asked curtly. "I've never been greatly addicted to the use of euphemisms and evasions, and if I thought you were responsible for something I wouldn't hesitate to tell you. To be any good, it has to work both ways."

"I know. But aside from the fact I don't think it's true—"

"Thank you. You *are* nice, Mr. Ingram. But you haven't heard the story."

"No." He resumed pumping. "But there's more to it than his thinking you tried to kill him. Why is he so afraid of water?"

"Because he thinks that's the *way* we tried to kill him, by drowning—"

He shook his head. "No. It's still not that simple." He told her briefly of Rae's throwing the whisky bottle overboard and of Warriner's reaction to watching it sink.

She nodded. "Yes. I know about that part of it." She was silent for a moment, thinking. "I'm not sure I can explain it myself, except that I think it's a fear of drowning carried to the point of phobia. You know what acrophobia is, of course?"

"Yes. A morbid fear of heights. But it has nothing to do with water."

"I know. But in his case I think it does." She nodded toward the sea around them. "When you look out there you see nothing but the surface. So do I; so does everybody. We realize vaguely that two miles down there's a bottom, but we never think of it, even if we're swimming in it— probably even if we're in trouble in it. It makes no difference whether you drown in seven feet of water, or seven miles; you still drown within a few feet of the surface. But you're *in* the water; I think he imagines himself rather precariously suspended on the surface of it, as if it were a film of some kind, ten thousand feet above the bottom. In other words, I get the impression he sees it all the way down. Hence, acrophobia. As I say, I'm only guessing, but how else can you account for that horror when he sees something sinking below him? To him, it's not sinking; it's *falling*. And, like all people with acrophobia, he imagines himself falling with it."

Ingram nodded, though still not convinced she was right. "But he wasn't always like that?"

"Oh, no. He was an excellent swimmer. And skin-diver. It's simply because of what we did to him ten days ago. But you have to understand what happened before, and what the situation was. Explosive is a good one-word description. To begin with, not one of us was competent to take a yacht across the Pacific, and incompetence multiplied by any number up to infinity is still incompetence. Four people who don't know what they're doing—"

"Are simply four times worse than one," Ingram said. "So nobody was in charge?"

"No. Not after things started to fall apart. Hughie, as legal owner of the yacht and the only one with any sailing experience at all, should have been in command, but you can't force a man to command, to fight back, to accept responsibility, if the only responsibility he's ever had in his life was to be acceptable and pleasing to a succession of overprotective women who took care of him. And if you happen to be in love with him and have to stand there helplessly day after day and watch this disintegration under pressure, this thing you can't do anything about, eventually your own frustration may goad you into doing something stupid and cruel and unforgivable. But I didn't intend to make excuses, and I'm getting ahead of the story anyway."

[12]

"HUGHIE," SHE WENT ON, "HAS ALWAYS BEEN OBSESSED by a feeling for the greatness of Gauguin, and it's been a lifelong ambition of his to go to Polynesia and live among the islands as he did, escape from the rat race the same way, paint the same subjects, experience the same things. So, when we were married in Europe almost a year ago, I let myself be persuaded, in spite of the fact I had some misgivings about it. In the first place, there's no escape from our so-called civilization any more; the twentieth century is something we're locked into and there's no way we can get out; when we got to Papeete we'd probably find the same jukeboxes, the same headlines, the same cocktail parties, the same jet service from here to there, the same Bomb, and the same exhortations to embrace the finer life by buying something. And in the second place, I was more than a little doubtful of our ability to sail a boat down there. But at heart I wanted to be persuaded, and I was. From my point of view there were several things in favor of it. No doubt you can guess what some of them were, but in the interests of clarity they might as well be included in this confession. I'm considerably older than Hughie, and when I met him I was a widow, a fairly wealthy one. You know what he looks like. The picture is trite to the point of banality, except that in this case it's not true at all. He's no glorified beach-boy, and we were genuinely in love with each other. And while I bleed very little over the opinions of other people, I didn't want him regarded as something he wasn't—at least, not yet, by the grace of God. I have a small but very good collection of paintings, and I know the work of talent when I see it. I wanted to help him, and in Hughie's case one way of helping him—and me—was to keep him out of the reach of all that gaggle of *soi-disant* benefactresses and panting patrons of the arts who couldn't keep their hands off him."

She broke off with an impatient gesture and then went on. "But enough of that. Hughie bought and studied all the books he could find on yachting and navigation. We chartered a yacht, with a professional crew of two, for a cruise in the western Mediterranean, from Cannes down to the Balearics, to learn as much as we could from practical experience. We came back to the States last winter, bought *Orpheus,* and began getting ready."

She smiled musingly. "Then I think we were betrayed. No doubt you remember the old ploy of crooked gamblers, letting the sheep, the intended victim, win the first few hands in order to increase the stakes. It was as if the Pacific Ocean, or fate, did it deliberately. The passage from Santa Barbara down to La Paz was ridiculously easy. Nothing went wrong at all. The weather was perfect, Hughie's navigation was seemingly accurate enough, the couple with us, who were old friends of mine from San Francisco, were congenial, and we were never at sea long enough for the confinement and too close association to cause any friction, because we made stops at San Diego and Ensenada. If anything had gone wrong in that first leg of the trip we would have been brought face to face with our own inexperience and incompetence, and we'd have had sense enough to give it up. But nothing did, and we were far too overconfident and cocky by the time we reached La Paz.

"Then the other couple had to abandon the trip there and go back to San Francisco because of illness. We lay at anchor in the harbor for nearly three months."

"Were you living aboard all the time?" Ingram asked.

"No. We came back to California, by plane, for several weeks, and part of the time we lived ashore at a hotel. Why?"

"I think that's when the dry rot began to run wild. *Orpheus* may have still been sound enough to make it to Papeete when you left Santa Barbara, but after three months of lying there in La Paz, probably with no ventilation below, she was eaten up with it by the time you sailed."

She nodded. "At any rate, we were stranded. *Orpheus*

was too large for two people to handle, even if we'd dared attempt it alone. None of my friends who would have liked to go could get away. We wrote to the yacht broker who'd sold us the boat, and he managed to locate a professional willing to make the trip, a man named Grover or Glover, who turned out to be utterly impossible. He arrived on the plane from Tijuana dead drunk, and somehow managed to stay that way the five days he was in La Paz, without, as far as we could discover, ever taking a drink. And while it might have been interesting from the medical point of view to see if he could stay bagged all the way across the Pacific with no visible intake of alcohol, as a yacht captain he was hopeless. We paid him off and decanted him into the Tijuana plane. So we were on the point of selling *Orpheus* and flying to Papeete to buy another boat there where we could hire an Island crew, when we met the Bellews at the little hotel ashore. Bellew was gathering material for an article on big-game fishing in the Gulf of California, and we became quite friendly in the two weeks they were there. We asked them to make the trip with us."

It was a tragic mistake, but one that had been very easy to make. It was banal to say that Bellew had seemed different ashore, but in the end that was what it amounted to. She supposed they all had, for that matter. Bellew was a man it was easy to get along with sitting around a café table sipping tall iced drinks in a backwater fishing port as limited in other diversions and other friends as La Paz. He'd led an intense and active outdoor life and had a great fund of entertaining stories which he told exceedingly well and with only a little suggestion of boasting. He played the guitar and sang folk songs in the manner of Burl Ives, and he and Hughie, who also sang very well, had two or three times put on highly successful impromptu shows for the other patrons of the hotel. He was big and outgoing and, if a little loud at times, not offensively so, and there was a male competence and assurance about him she'd instinctively trusted because they somehow reminded her of her first husband. It would take more trying circumstances than sitting in cafés or fishing for marlin with him to bring up the other side of the coin, the cruelty and the contempt for any kind of weakness.

Perhaps, on the other hand, Bellew could feel with some justification that he'd been fooled too. He'd claimed no experience with the sea except that highly specialized business of big-game fishing, in power cruisers and usually very near to land, while Hughie, emboldened by the complete success of the trip down the coast from Santa Barbara, had perhaps sounded a little too salty and seagoing, sitting around the drinks.

And she'd liked Estelle Bellew—at least at first. Estelle was a rather shy and only moderately attractive woman of around forty, who was completely wrapped up in her photography and had no apparent designs on Hughie. This turned out to be another mistake, of course. While she didn't have any amatory interest in him—then or later— she did have a great reservoir of unexpended gentleness and compassion she'd never had any occasion to use, living with this hairy and domineering bastard she was married to, and she was possessed of an equally frustrated mother instinct that Hughie brought out in full, especially after it became apparent how badly Hughie needed a mother or somebody to protect him from the Pacific Ocean and from Bellew's abrasive contempt.

"Why did he want to make the trip?" Ingram asked. "Bellew, I mean."

"I don't even know who first suggested it," she replied. "It was just one of those ideas that can burst on the scene fully grown when four people are sitting in a bar with their second or third round of drinks. It was about ten days after we'd met them, and we'd just come in from a day's fishing as his guests on the boat he'd chartered. He already had all the material for the story he was doing on the fishing at La Paz and was sure he could get a story, or perhaps two, out of the trip. I told him we would be glad to pay their air transportation back from Papeete. And, after all, it would only take a month." She smiled bitterly. "We sailed from La Paz twenty-six days ago."

Before they were more than a week out, everything began to go wrong. They blew out a sail in a squall and lost another overboard. Leaks began to show up from opened deck seams so that when they were shipping any water aboard everything below was soaked. They missed Clipperton Island because something had apparently slipped up in Hughie's navigation. They used up most of their fuel trying to beat their way back to it, which was ridiculous, since it was uninhabited anyway, but by now they were no longer acting rationally but only motivated by their endless quarrels. They gave up trying to find the island after it failed a second and third time to appear where Hughie said it was. *Orpheus* began to leak alarmingly, so it took more pumping every day to keep the water out of the cabins.

But beyond all that, it was the old story of clashing personalities jammed into too small a space with nowhere to go to avoid each other. Bellew became caustic, loud-mouthed, and finally insufferable, openly contemptuous of Hughie's mistakes in navigation and seamanship, while Hughie, instead of fighting back, retreated into sullenness and pouting. Estelle Bellew was sympathetic and tried to shield him from her husband. Lillian herself lashed out at Bellew in defense of Hughie—or she did at first, until she decided that wasn't the answer—but at the same time it was lacerating to have to admit to herself that he even needed defending against another man. Some of her hurt and resentment must have showed, for Hughie began turning increasingly to Estelle rather than to her for comfort when he backed down from Bellew. And Estelle tried increasingly to help him, as though he were a boy, and alone.

"That in itself was infuriating," she went on. "The implication was that I was some species of heartless monster who had no sympathy, no feeling for him at all. She had the best intentions in the world, but she simply couldn't seem to understand that that was the trouble in the first place, that he'd never in his life had to accept the responsibility for his own actions or fight for his rights, because there was always some woman panting to shield him from the one and buy him the other. And she was simply doing it again. I was trying to help him in the only way he could be helped—or that I *hoped* he could be helped—by letting him work it out for himself, no matter how I cringed and wanted to go somewhere and cry when he simply retreated into petulance in the face of Bellew's contempt, or no matter how much easier it would have been to set him behind me and then remove Bellew's skin in strips. So I began to treat her—Estelle—with the same insufferable nastiness that Bellew treated Hughie.

"In the end I couldn't stand it any longer—the helplessness of it, I mean—watching Hughie being browbeaten without the spirit to fight back, and not being able to do anything in the world about it except drive him more and more to some other woman for sympathy. I hated both of them, and I hated myself. I blew up. I did the one thing that was guaranteed to hurt everybody. I made an open, deliberate pass at Bellew."

"Well, it's been done before," Ingram said.

"But seldom by people who are assumed to be adult. And seldom with consequences as tragic. It happened one night just at the end of the second week."

It was shortly after dinner and they were all on deck. She was at the wheel, having relieved Hughie just at dusk so he could take a series of star sights while he could still see the horizon. Bellew was sprawled in the cockpit beyond her, while Estelle was sitting alone on the forward end of the deckhouse, looking at the fading afterglow of sunset. Hughie's star sights didn't work out. He'd got three of them, with three lines of position several hundred miles apart, none of which crossed, or were anywhere near the dead-reckoning position based on the equally dubious fix he'd got at noon. Either his figures were wrong or he'd mistaken his stars. A long time went by while he checked and rechecked his work. Then he came out on deck with a star chart, but in the meantime the moon had risen and the stars were fading and hard to distinguish. And Bellew started on him again. Her flesh crawled.

"How's it look, Magellan? We still seem to be in the same ocean?"

Hughie made no reply. He went on futilely trying to match up at least one of the stars with his chart. Her heart ached for him. She wished she could help him. And why, oh why, in the name of God, didn't he turn on the badgering and idiotic *salaud* and tell him to shut up?

"I'll tell you what, Commodore," Bellew went on, "if it turns out we're anywhere near Greeley, Colorado, I got a friend runs a bar there. . . ."

She closed her eyes. Do *something,* Hughie!

He did. Like a sullen child, he threw the star chart on the deck. "Hughie," she called out quickly, trying to save him from utter shame, "let me try. Maybe I could help—" But without even a glance at her he'd already turned and gone forward to Estelle. She could see the two of them sitting close together in the light of the rising moon. She'd bitten her lip to keep from crying, and she could taste blood in her mouth. Then out of some dark and insensate desire to wound them all, herself included, she said to Bellew, "We don't seem to be entirely necessary, do we? But it is a beautiful night, and if you'd like help with some of *your* problems, why don't you bring up a couple of drinks?"

The others had seen, all right—at least the merged silhouette against the moon—and heard the laughter and the singing. One of them was dead now, and the other was mad, at least partly as the result of it, so she was the only one left—besides Bellew, of course—with any true and rational appreciation of the scene as something to be treasured forever. It had taken perhaps fifteen minutes to sicken herself to the point where she had to go below or jump overboard. She removed the repulsive hand from inside her bra, got up, leaving the wheel untended, and went down to the cabin and locked the door. Hughie never came down at all. Apparently he'd slept on deck.

She went on in a minute. "So there you have the situation. We had everything we needed now for disaster, or for something very messy, but when it came, two days later, it was only an accident.

"I'll try to give it to you in chronological sequence, as we reconstructed it afterward, though it concerned four people in different places, I was asleep through a good part of it, and at the end only two of us were still alive and able to give a coherent account of what had happened. It was two p.m., and we'd been lying becalmed for over an hour, with all sail still set, but the booms sheeted in to keep them from banging. It was Bellew's wheel watch, and he was sitting in the cockpit, keeping an eye out for signs of a breeze. Estelle Bellew was lying in her bunk in the forward cabin, reading, I think, and Hughie and I were in our cabin aft. I was pretending to be asleep; that way we had at least the semblance of an excuse for the fact we weren't speaking to each other. Hughie went out.

"He came on deck. Bellew, of course, was in the cockpit. Neither of them spoke. Hughie went over to the rail and was looking down into the water when he saw the school of dolphin which had been following the boat and playing around under it for the past two days. These are dolphin, the fish, you understand, and not porpoises."

Ingram nodded. "Very beautiful fish, like flame under water. The Mexicans call them *dorado*—golden, or gilded. They like to lie under anything floating on the surface."

"They're the ones. Anyway, while we were looking at them he remembered that Estelle had said she'd like to see if she could photograph them from below the surface if the school was ever around when we were becalmed. So, still without speaking to Bellew, he went back below. Only, when he passed through the deckhouse, he went forward first into the main cabin—that is, the saloon—and called out to Estelle through the curtained passage at the forward end of it, telling her about the fish. She was eager to try to photograph them, so she said she'd put on a swim suit and meet him on deck. Bellew, still aft in the cockpit, heard none of this, of course. Hughie then went back up into the deckhouse and on down into our cabin to put on his swim trunks and get a diving mask and snorkel. But I didn't know it, because by this time I *was* asleep.

"Hughie was below probably only a few minutes, but when he came back up through the deckhouse and stepped on deck Bellew was no longer there. He'd gone below, into the main cabin, to make a sandwich. This, of course, is forward, toward the Bellews' cabin, so—since the two of them hadn't met in the deckhouse—Bellew had no idea

Hughie had returned to the deck. Fortunately, you know the layout below, and you can understand why we had to reconstruct this whole thing afterward to try to understand how it could have happened."

Ingram nodded. He could see the tragedy already beginning to take form, like the choreography of some death scene in a ballet, where every movement had to fit.

She went on. "In another minute or two Estelle came on deck from the forward hatch, the one leading up directly from their cabin. She had on her swim suit and was carrying a snorkel and mask and an underwater camera. That is, it wasn't really an underwater camera with a housing, but one of her thirty-five-millimeter cameras that she'd made a watertight bag for with some kind of clear plastic and carried slung around her neck on a cord. Hughie put the ladder over just forward of amidships, and they eased down it into the water—not jumping or diving in because they didn't want to frighten the dolphin.

"It was a rule, of course, since all of us did swim when we had the chance, that nobody should ever go in the water without notifying whoever was on watch. But Hughie apparently thought, since Bellew was gone from the deck, that he was forward in his own cabin and that Estelle had told him before she came up. And Estelle, since Hughie had been the one who'd brought up the whole thing, must have assumed that Hughie had notified him. She hadn't even seen Bellew, because he was in the main cabin. So they put on their masks and snorkels and began trying to get close to the school of fish, which was now moving away from the boat. There was a moderate groundswell running, so even when Bellew came back on deck he probably wouldn't have seen them unless he'd happened to be looking in their direction at the moment they rose to the top or the near side of a swell.

"Hughie has never been completely rational since, and when I saw him again, six hours later, he was raving and incoherent, but as well as I could piece it together they'd been in the water about ten minutes and were not over a hundred yards from the boat when it happened. They were fairly close to the dolphin and they'd both dived, Hughie just looking at them while Estelle tried to snap a picture. Hughie came up first, and when his head was above water he was aware that something had changed. It was a second or two before he realized what it was. A breeze was blowing across his face. He turned and looked toward *Orpheus* and screamed. But Bellew didn't hear him.

"As I said, this was at two p.m. I awoke a little after three-thirty and could tell from the angle of heel and the lessened rolling that we'd picked up a breeze while I was asleep and were under way. I noticed Hughie wasn't in his bunk, but paid no attention to it. In a few minutes I got up, dressed, washed my face, and went up through the deckhouse to the main cabin to brew a cup of tea. It was ten minutes of four when I carried it out on deck. Bellew was at the wheel, of course. We were on the starboard tack and probably making around two knots in a breeze that didn't much more than fill the sails.

"Bellew merely grunted when I sat down in the cockpit, but in a minute he said, 'Did you call the great Magellan? Or are you going to take his watch?'

"That was the first second it dawned on me I hadn't seen him anywhere. I jumped up, spilling the tea, and ran below, and I was all the way down in the main cabin before I realized that if he *had* gone to that woman's cabin, if he'd been silly enough to go in there with her husband on deck, I'd already given it away and Bellew would probably beat him to death. I spoke outside the curtain. There was no answer, so I pulled it back. The cabin was empty. I pounded on the door of the washroom and opened it. There was no one in it, nor in the one aft."

She was whimpering and numb with terror by the time she made it back to the deck and saw the ladder hanging over the side. Bellew already had the wheel hard over, and *Orpheus* was coming ponderously about.

She had got her voice back at last and was shrieking at him as she set up the weather runner and trimmed the jib sheet. *"When? How long ago?* You blind, stupid, forgetful fool, you've killed them!"

"Shut up!" Bellew ordered curtly. "They didn't tell me."

"Well, you must have seen them! You were supposed to be on deck!" She broke off then, realizing at last that they were wasting precious seconds on this idiocy when there was so much to be done. They had to figure out the reciprocal of the course he'd been making and estimate the distance they'd come since the breeze sprang up. And none of it was easy. The wind had been erratic, and he'd had to tack twice when it headed him. Their speed had varied from an estimated less than one knot to an estimated three and a half. None of it had been written down because he'd intended to write a rough average of it in the log when he was relieved. She took the wheel, heading back in the approximate direction, while he struggled with the figures. In around ten minutes he had it calculated as closely as they ever would—somewhere to the east-northeast, four to five miles.

She began to hope again. It was only two hours, and they were both good swimmers. Hughie, she knew, could stay afloat four hours easily, and they would have been swimming this way—no, he couldn't even see the masts at this distance, not down in the water. But for at least half the time he would have been able to see them, anyway each time he came to the top of a swell. It was still three hours and more till dark, and she'd get Bellew to hoist her to the top of the mainmast in a bosun's chair. They'd get there in time. Then the breeze began to falter. It came on again for three or four minutes, dropped once more, and then died completely.

They couldn't run the engine. They'd already used up all the fuel. They lay helplessly in the trough and rolled.

They launched the dinghy. Bellew wanted to go because he could row faster, but she insisted. She was two hundred yards away before she realized she didn't have the faintest idea which direction she was going in. She came back and got a compass and set it between her feet, even though she knew it was hopeless looking for them in the dinghy. She was too low in the water to see anything or to be seen. She was far out from *Orpheus* when the sun went down and it began to grow dark. She stood up in the dinghy, calling his name until she could no longer see anything but the distant gleam of the masthead light Bellew had turned on. She rowed back and went aboard. She lay in the cabin in the darkness, trying not to think of what it must have been like to see the boat sailing away from him a thousand miles from land. Bellew came in and tried to speak to her. She didn't even know what he said. He went away, into the forward cabin.

About half an hour later she heard him run through the deckhouse on the way to the deck, shouting, "I heard something." She ran up. The spreader lights were on, as well as the masthead light, but they were glowing only faintly, scarcely brighter than candles, because the batteries were discharged. She ran back into the deckhouse for a flashlight. She began throwing its beam out across the water. Then she heard the sound too, a faint whimpering, but it was coming from aboard rather than from the water. She threw the light forward.

Hughie had come up the ladder and was lying at the foot of the mainmast, his arms locked around it, his face pressed against the wood. His shoulders shook, and he was still making that not quite human sound deep in his throat. She noticed, in that way you sometimes fix your attention on details in moments of overwhelming emotion, that there was a gaping and bluish cut, no longer bleeding, across the knuckles of his right hand. He was alone. Estelle hadn't come back.

"As weak as he was after six hours in the water," she went on, "it took both of us to pry his arms loose from the mast. We half led and half carried him below and put him on his bunk. He opened his eyes; at first they were completely blank, and then he began to recognize us. He cringed back and jumped off the bunk and cowered back in a corner, screaming at us. He was almost incoherent, but we could understand bits of what he was saying. We'd tried to kill him. We'd gone off and left him deliberately. I was only pretending to be asleep and knew he'd gone into the water. And there was something about a shark, over and over.

"In the end, Bellew had to hold him while I injected a

sedative dose of morphine in his arm. He fought us, and when he felt the prick of the needle he screamed.

"He never let either of us come near him again. He slept, if he ever slept at all, in the sail locker up forward, with the door barricaded inside. He looked rational, at least most of the time, but he was silent and withdrawn. He would never approach the rail without that look of horror on his face and a death grip on something solid, like a man with acrophobia frozen to a girder a thousand feet above the street. When we'd try to question him about Estelle, he'd go all to pieces and begin shouting again about a shark. I made Bellew stop asking him. It was three days before I got a more or less coherent story of what had happened.

"They'd been attacked by a shark. He still had his mask on, and he swam down and hit it on the snout with his fist, trying to drive it away. That was the way he got that wound on his hand. It had avoided him because he was under the water, but had come up and gone for Estelle, who was threshing on the surface. It cut her in two. There was nothing he could do. He swam out of the bloody water and got away, but the sight of it was too much—that and the fear, and the belief we'd done it deliberately. He cracked up."

So Bellew was right, Ingram thought. He was on the point of asking if she believed the story herself, but realized the futility of it. If she did believe it, it was only because she refused to accept the truth. She, better than any of them, should know what Hughie was really running from, but if she had already made the choice and was determined to accept the blame, argument was useless, and there were more urgent things to think about at the moment. No doubt a psychiatrist could dig it out of her and force her to acknowledge it, but he wasn't a psychiatrist, they were on a sinking boat in mid-ocean, and nine-tenths of his mind was occupied with the cold and relentless struggle to keep the thought of Rae from swamping it. And, in the end, perhaps the specific act for which she blamed herself wasn't significant anyway. The guilt she accepted was the blanket indictment of having been the link at which the lengthening chain of Hughie-protection had finally snapped. She'd been minding the baby when it crawled into the goldfish pond and drowned.

It was possible, of course, that Hughie did think—or had managed to convince himself—that they'd deliberately gone off and left the two of them to die. And naturally he might have an irrational fear of water, after having been in it for six hours in mid-ocean, part of the time in the dark and thinking of the bottom ten thousand feet below him. But neither of these was the horror he was trying to escape, the thing he saw when something was sinking in the water below him. That was Estelle. The only part of it that was difficult to understand was what sick compulsion had kept him there, looking down through the mask at her body falling into the depths after he had killed her.

He'd seen the wound on Hughie's hand. And it wasn't an abrasion such as he'd have received from striking the sandpapery skin of a shark. It was a cut. It had been caused by human teeth, or the broken glass of a diving mask.

So Estelle had panicked and tried to climb up on him to get out of the water, the way the drowning often did. He'd beaten her off with his fists and knocked her out. And the ironic part of it was that, for anybody willing to accept at least a portion of the blame, there'd still have been a way out. Subduing the panicky person who was threatening to drown both himself and his rescuer was an accepted part of lifesaving. Somebody else might have convinced himself he'd hit her only to try to save her, so he could turn her on her back and tow her, and then she'd slipped away from him and drowned before he could get her back to the surface. But not Hughie, who couldn't accept any of the penalty for anything. He'd had to invent his nonexistent shark, which even he couldn't believe. But he *had* to believe it, and go on believing it, or face an unpleasant fact for the first time in his life. And, for a beginner, he'd been handed a rough one to face.

She must have still had the camera slung around her neck. Those 35 mm. jobs were heavy for their size, and with none of the built-in buoyancy from a standard underwater housing it must have been just enough to tip the scales beyond that state of near equilibrium of a woman's body in salt water—any woman except the very thin and muscular and heavy-boned—and keep her falling straight below him after she was unconscious. Even then, the rate of descent was probably very slow, at least until she was down to where the pressure began collapsing her chest cavity. And Hughie had watched her.

No, he thought then, not necessarily. Maybe he'd only imagined watching her; maybe it had already begun in his mind. At any rate, there was the horror, and there was the beginning of that awareness of depth, or of height, upon which he was impaled—seeing the body of this friend, this woman who'd been so good to him and whom he'd killed in panic to save his own life, slide into the ever-deepening abyss below him, still clearly visible at fifty feet, a hundred, maybe a hundred and fifty, and after she had dwindled and disappeared entirely he could go on imagining it—a thousand feet, five thousand, ten thousand, and still falling.

Jesus, he thought, I'm glad I'm carrying it around looking for a place to set it down.

He was aware then that *Orpheus*'s motion was changing. The groundswell was becoming confused as it encountered the mounting seas built up in the squall. He glanced out toward the dark turbulence of the sky in the northeast and the advancing wall of rain that was probably less than two miles away.

"Maybe you'd better call Bellew," he said.

[13]

WITHOUT ANY REMEMBRANCE AT ALL OF HOW SHE'D GOT there she was standing on the companion ladder, looking out into blazing sunlight and the encircling blue of the sea.

Ten feet in front of her the golden impervious head was poised above the binnacle, and she could hear herself shrieking through the clatter of the engine.

"Go back! For the love of God, go back before something awful happens! Don't make it happen, don't make it, *please don't make it!"* Her voice skidded up over the rim into hysteria and incoherence.

There was no reply. He glanced at her briefly and then back at the compass with something of the studied avoidance of a diner looking the other way after a waiter has dropped a tray of food, as though he was as disappointed in this uncouth screeching as he had been in her selfishness. Then, with no clear idea how she'd got there either, she was back in the forward cabin, holding onto the upright pipe of the bunk frame with one hand while she ran the fingers of the other across the side of her face and upward into her hair. Something was quivering, either her face or the hand, but she wasn't sure which, any more than she was sure whether she'd actually gone out there and screamed the warning at him or whether she'd just imagined it. No, she must have gone out, because the door was unlatched and open. She could hear it banging behind her as *Saracen* rolled.

The shotgun still lay on the bunk where she'd dropped it, the three separate, improbable pieces suddenly united and frozen into this unmistakable shape of deadliness. She jerked her eyes away from it and looked at her watch, and then a second time in disbelief. It was 12:45 p.m. Time was hurtling past her, and she was beginning to lose whole intervals of it. They were already twenty miles from that sinking boat, and by sunset, when they'd be over fifty, she would have cracked completely. Her chin still quivering, she looked around the tiny compartment again, seeing for the twentieth time only the walls of the trap, this corner she'd been backed into and from which there was no escape except one. She'd tried everything else, and it was hopeless. He was impregnable, unreachable—

Then, with the suddenness of a thrown switch, the wildness and despair were gone, and she was strangely calm. It was as if her mind had come into focus at last, with everything else dropping away until there remained only the two simple, elemental facts she'd been groping for all the time, the only two that mattered at all. John was going to die unless she saved him. And she had the means to do it.

At first she thought the engine had stopped, it had grown so quiet. But when she listened, she could still hear it; it was just farther away, and there was a faint rushing or ringing sound inside her head, as if she had been taking quinine. It was like being enclosed in some huge bubble that protected her from all extraneous sound or thought or interference. It was cold inside the bubble, and there didn't seem to be enough air, because her breathing was rapid and very shallow, but she was invulnerable to everything beyond. She went over and picked up the shotgun.

And this was strange too, with some feeling that she'd done it before and knew exactly what she had to do. It was as if, while her conscious mind was recoiling from it in revulsion, some far level of the unconscious had already accepted the gun with complete fatalism and calmly planned its use. She had to learn how it worked. She pointed it away from her and tried to pull the triggers. Nothing happened. But she'd expected that. Guns had safety mechanisms of some kind so they couldn't be fired accidentally. She began searching for the key to it, and found it immediately, since it was the only part of the weapon not already identified. It had to be this small oblong button just back of the lever that broke it open at the breech so you could put in the shells. She tried to push the button down, but nothing happened. Then it must slide. She pushed it forward, and it did, perhaps a quarter of an inch. She pulled the triggers and heard the clicks, one after the other, as hammers fell on the firing pins.

The shells. Still inviolate within her bubble of cold and unswerving concentration, she went out into the after cabin and knelt before the drawer. There were two boxes of them. Both had been wrapped in plastic and then covered with two or three coats of varnish to protect them from the humidity of the tropics. She'd need a knife. She was making a note of this and reaching over the medicine kit for one of the boxes of shells, when she paused. It was only for a minor part of a second, a fleeting but inexplicable hiatus of movement that was noticeable at all only because ever since she'd accepted this thing and committed herself she'd been going forward with the inevitability of some machine running downhill on rails.

Poised there on the dead center of this almost imperceptible hesitation, with the feeling that somebody was pounding on the wall of the bubble, trying to get in or to attract her attention, she looked down into the drawer, wondering what had caused it. Besides some heavy clothing they wouldn't need until they got down into the higher latitudes, it held only those articles which, in addition to the shotgun, had to be sealed in port by customs—the shells; her cigarettes; John's cigars; the medicine kit, because of the narcotics it contained; and several bottles of whisky and two or three of rum. Then the feeling was gone. The protective concentration closed in around her again, and she was moving ahead. She gathered up the box of shells, picked up a small paring knife from a galley drawer, and hurried back.

It took several minutes to hack her way into the box. She extracted two of the shells and set the box on the deck under the bunk. She broke the gun at the breech with the lever, dropped them in, and closed it. She was fortunate in that her very lack of familiarity with guns spared her the deadly association of those three sounds linked in sequence—the *toinnnk, toinnnk,* of the shells dropping into the ends of the tubular air columns of the barrels, and the metallic click as the breech closed and locked.

But she wasn't so lucky with the blanket. Strangely, the blanket was worse now than the gun, and it might have stopped her except for the furious intensity of her concentration and the momentum she had already gathered. Because she knew what she had to do with it, and do immediately and without hesitation or thought; if she waited, she might never go up there at all, and the act would have been for nothing.

She set the gun down on one of the sailbags, peeled the blanket from the bunk, and held it up before her by the corners with her face averted, like a fisherman approaching a blaze behind a shield. The ocean of sickness beyond the bubble surged inward and threatened to collapse it, but she looked down at her feet, her mind shored up against everything but the problem, and decided she could get up the ladder this way and across the cockpit.

She retrieved the gun, took the blanket in her other arm, and went out. The roaring in her head was louder now, so she could scarcely hear the engine. She was cold all over and wasn't sure she was breathing at all; there seemed to be some tremendous weight pressing on her chest. She walked with a stiff-legged artificial gait, like a mechanical toy, fighting the rubbery weakness of her knees, but she was still going forward, still protected and invulnerable. She could see nothing on either side of her. Straight ahead, as if at the end of a long tunnel, the bright oblong patch of sunlight fell through the open hatch, sweeping back and forth across the ladder as *Saracen* rolled. She reached it. She stepped up on the first tread of the ladder and peered out.

She could just see over the hatch coaming, and only his face was visible as he sat in the after end of the cockpit behind the wheel. He was looking down into the compass, and his lips were moving, apparently without sound, though she didn't know for sure because of the engine noise and that roaring in her ears. He glanced up then, straight into her eyes, but there was no recognition, no indication he even saw her. He looked back at the compass, his lips continuing to move. Somewhere inside her a voice was screaming: *Now, now!*

She dropped the blanket beside her on the ladder and brought up the gun, pushing the safety button forward. The barrels reached up and out, resting on the coaming in front of her, and when she put her shoulder against the stock and sighted along them they were pointing just slightly to one side of his face. She moved them over, and when she closed her left eye they were lined up, foreshortened and centered on his forehead ten feet in front of her. She could no longer breathe at all. Her right index finger, like some great unwieldy sausage, came in against the gun, felt the forward edge of the trigger guard, slipped back around it, inside, and lay against the trigger. All she had to do was pull. She tried.

She closed both eyes and let her head fall forward, wanting help from somewhere, but there was no help; she was alone, and if it was to be done she had to do it. When she opened her eyes and looked along the barrels again, the beautiful, hated, mad, impervious head was still there on the ends of them like a permanent decoration installed in a moment of gruesome whimsy by some gunsmith gone mad himself. She tried once more to pull the trigger, and then came down from the ladder with the gun, remembering just in time to push the safety back before she sank down at the foot of it. She couldn't even cry. There were no tears left.

In a few minutes she had strength enough again to gather up the gun and blanket and go back inside the forward cabin with them. She unloaded the gun, dropped it on the bunk, and put the two shells back in the box. That ended it. She knew now. Not even to save John's life could she assassinate in cold blood a boy who didn't know what he was doing.

Or had she actually proved that? she wondered. Maybe all she'd really proved was that she couldn't do it now, at one p.m., still five hours before the deadline, the point of no return. What about then, when she knew she was renouncing all hope of ever seeing him again? But she was too tired, too emptied to think about it now. She had to rest. She sat down on the edge of the bunk, and almost immediately, as the tension uncoiled inside her, she remembered that strange pause or hesitation when she was reaching into the drawer for the shells. Something had been trying to get her attention through the protective armor of concentration. What was it?

It had to be one of the things she'd seen in the drawer. The medicine kit! That was it. But why? Was there some connection with that story Warriner had told about the deaths from botulism and his vain attempts to treat it? No-o. But, wait. She had it then. The narcotics! Hope blossomed, and then just as suddenly it was gone and she sank back into the depths. Of course there was morphine in the kit, and a hypodermic syringe, but what good was it? It was hardly likely Warriner was going to let her stick a needle in his arm and inject him full of opiates. She stopped. Inject? No. There was something else. Then she sat upright. *Codeine!* There was a bottle of codeine tablets in it.

She ran out into the after cabin and yanked open the drawer. The medicine kit was in a wooden box with a hinged cover. She threw the cover up and began searching hurriedly through the bottles, plastic vials, and small cardboard cartons. Aspirin, paregoric, iodine, aureomycin, alcohol, sulfa, sutures—here, this was it. It was a small, square-shouldered bottle with a screw top, its neck stuffed with cotton. She lifted it out and read the typewritten label. *"One tablet for relief of pain. Do not repeat within six hours."*

There seemed to be fifteen or twenty in it. One, she thought, would make you very drowsy, depending on individual tolerance. She had no idea what a lethal dose would be, but probably anything above four or five might be fatal even to a young man in the prime of life such as Warriner. She didn't want to kill him, even in this painless and unmessy way, but on the other hand too small a dose would be worse than none at all. It would only warn him that he'd been drugged. Three, she thought; that should be safe enough both ways. But how to administer it?

In food, or in something to drink? There'd probably be less chance of his suspecting anything if it were in something to eat. She could pulverize three of them, mix the powder with canned potted ham or something equally spicy to cover the taste, and make a sandwich of it. No, she thought then. The chances were he was going to be suspicious of *anything* she offered him. Irrational he might be, but he was no fool. She thought for a moment. Then she saw the answer, and she smiled for the first time in four hours.

She slammed the drawer shut and strode back to the galley section of the cabin. Having shaken three of the tablets from the bottle, she set them on the tiny drainboard shelf next to the sink and reached up into the stowage racks for a glass. She took two teaspoons from a drawer, set one of the tablets in one spoon and used the heel of the other to crush it, pressing them between her fingers. She dropped the resultant powder in the glass and was reaching for the second tablet when she felt *Saracen* go into a hard left turn and at the same time roll down to starboard. Both the glass and the bottle of codeine tablets started to slide. She caught the glass, but the bottle escaped her and fell on deck. It didn't break, but it rolled and slid all the way across to the starboard side, spilling the tablets as it went. She set the glass in the sink, so it couldn't roll off too, and went lunging after the bottle. She had it and was down on her knees picking up the scattered tablets at the foot of the companion ladder when Warriner screamed just above her. He was already in the hatch, coming down the ladder.

She sprang to her feet and wheeled to run, but it was too late. When she slid through the doorway into the forward cabin he was right behind her and there was no time even to close the door. Trapped now, she turned, seeing the agony of his face and trying to will herself not to fight him. "It was a shark!" he cried out. He caught both her arms in a grip that made them hurt. "It was a shark!" And while she was still struggling with the panic inside her, she began to grasp that he hadn't come down here to attack her. He wanted help, comfort, something he thought she could give him, and if she could soothe him, or at least keep from antagonizing him, she might survive this crisis too. And it would be the last one. Then she remembered she still had the opened bottle of codeine tablets in her hand. She shoved the hand down beside her thigh to keep them out of sight.

"Don't you see, it was the shark!" Then *Saracen,* running at full throttle with no one at the wheel, careened off the side of a swell and went into another hard turn. They lost their balance in the welter of sailbags and cases of stores around the door, and she fell backward onto the bunk. She sat up. Warriner dropped to his knees between the bunks and pressed his face into her lap, encircling her legs with his arms. His shoulders shook. Her left hand was

DEAD CALM

free, but the other, holding the bottle, was trapped by his arms.

She reached down and gently stroked his head. "Of course it was the shark, Hughie."

He raised his head then and looked up at her, and while his eyes were still wild there was nothing dangerous in them. On the contrary, they were almost beseeching, like those of a frightened child. The words began to pour out, tumbling over each other. "It was a big hammerhead, over twelve feet long. I tried to drive it away. I tried to save her. I hit—I hit it on the nose. But she was up on the surface, splashing too much. If she'd come down where I was—they won't bother you under the water, you know that, everybody does—but she wouldn't dive. It was horrible, the shark cut her in two, the water was all bloody. . . ."

She had no idea what he was talking about, but what he wanted was plain enough. He was asking her for exoneration. It was the other boy who'd started the fight or had thrown the football through Mrs. Cramer's window. She stroked his head again. "It wasn't your fault, Hughie. Of course it was terrible, but you did everything you could."

His arms had relaxed their grip around her legs, and she was able to slide her right hand free. While he was still looking up at her face, she brought it up the side of her thigh and shoved the bottle into the pocket of her Bermuda shorts. She sighed. He hadn't seen it.

"You believe me, don't you?" he asked.

"Of course I believe you," she said.

"I knew you would. Somehow I knew it." He hugged her legs again, almost as if in gratitude, and pressed his face against her knees. His voice was almost normal as he went on, "You won't leave me, will you? It's so awful—" He stopped.

She glanced down. He had raised his head again, but this time he was looking at something behind her on the bunk. It was the shotgun. She felt the chill of gooseflesh spread up her back. He went on staring, and then he whispered, "You were going to kill me."

"No. Hughie, no. Listen—please, it's not even loaded."

He still hadn't moved, and his voice was no louder than before. "You want to kill me too."

He reached around behind her and slowly pulled it out by the barrels. There was nowhere she could run, nothing she could do. There wasn't even anything in her mind except the bitterness of the thought that after four hours she'd been within a few minutes of winning, and now she'd lost. Maybe the fear would come in a minute. She was simply too tired to handle more than one thing at a time.

With a wild outcry he lunged to his feet then and swung the gun against the side of the boat. The stock splintered and broke off against an oaken frame above and behind her head. She ducked down between the bunks as he swung again—not even at her, as far as she could tell, but merely in some fury of destruction directed against the gun itself. The barrels rang against the upright pipe of the bunk frame. He beat it twice more against the pipe and threw it behind him, into the after cabin. Above the noise of the engine she heard it slide and bounce along the deck and crash into something, probably the ladder at the after end. At the same moment, while he was turning and off balance, *Saracen* rolled down and the bow swung off on another violent change of course. He fell over against the bulkhead beside the door and slid down atop the sailbag behind which the compass was wedged. He was on his feet almost immediately, facing her. When she'd seen him lose his balance she'd started to scramble up, hoping to get out the door, but there wasn't time. He was right beside it. There was nowhere to go, anyway. She sat down on the bunk again, trying to conceal her fear. *Don't fight him,* she thought; don't try to run. Her only chance to survive was to use her weapons instead of his; there was a lost and frightened boy inside the maniac, and maybe she could reach him. And he could already have killed her with the gun barrels, but he hadn't.

He stared at her wildly for a moment and had taken a step toward her, when he turned, as if he'd remembered something. When he bent over the sailbag she knew what it was. He'd seen the compass when he fell, and the scratch pad with its penciled notations of the course. He lifted the compass out and with another cry of fury he turned and threw it against the starboard side of the cabin. The box splintered, and it fell to the deck in a ruin of broken glass and spilled alcohol.

Then, before he even had a chance to look back at her, she said gently, "Hughie, come here." When the frenzied eyes swung around and fastened on her, she touched her knees, where his head had rested before.

"You wanted to kill me!" he cried out. His hands clenched and opened, and he took a step toward her, coming between her and the door. She saw the hands come up level with her throat, but there was a faint uncertainty or hesitation in his movements now, and she'd detected just a trace of defiance in the outcry. Without that, perhaps she couldn't have found the self-control to do it. She continued to look up at him with perfect serenity.

"Don't be silly, Hughie," she said. "You know I wouldn't hurt you." She wasn't sure herself how she accomplished it, but the tone was squarely on pitch, the voice of all the mothers in the world, firm but still gentle, compassionate, and forgiving. She touched her knees again and said, "Come here, dear."

He came with a rush then. He fell to his knees before her with his face pressed against her legs, and he was crying uncontrollably.

The strength drained out of her, but she managed to remain erect while she gently stroked his head. The clatter of the engine went on. *Saracen* pitched, and the bow swung off onto another tangent in her blind flight across the surface of the sea. Part of it had been luck, she thought, in that the first, compulsive outburst had been directed against the shotgun, but she knew she could control him now. She had nothing more to fear from him. Except that she still couldn't make him go back. But the codeine would take care of that.

Then she remembered the compass and looked across to the opposite side of the cabin, where spilled alcohol still dripped down the planking of the hull. Well, she thought wearily, there must be some answer to that too; she'd think of it in a minute. Apparently after four hours of improvising and feeling your way along the rim of disaster you began to develop a belief there was always another handhold just beyond.

[14]

RUSSELL BELLEW HAD BEEN DREAMING HE WAS PACKING into the Bitterroot country again for elk when he awoke and he was back on that sinking abortion of a boat and the Duchess of California was poking his shoulder with a pair of rulers. She was looking down at him with that usual expression of hers, as if he were something that had just crawled out of the drain in a bus-station washroom. What the good Duchess needed, besides being knocked on her can a few times, was exactly what she'd have had this morning in about five more minutes if Goldilocks hadn't sighted that other boat and come charging down there with his club just as he got her pinned down on the bunk. Rub it on him for practice, would she?

"Madam called?" he asked.

"Ingram said to wake you."

He loved that bit with the rulers. He slid a hand up the back of her thigh and squeezed. "You should have used a longer stick."

"Obviously." There was no attempt to draw back, or hit him, and she didn't even bother to change expression. "Then you *are* awake?"

He sat up. "What does Hotspur want now?"

"There's a squall coming up."

"So?"

"So the bird of time has but a little way to fly—"

"Shove it."

She tore him off about three-sixteenths of another supercilious smile, dropped it in his eye, and said, "Yes, of course." She went back on deck.

Cuddly type, the good Duchess. But somebody should have warned her before this that nobody was quite as hard as she thought she was. No doubt she was a better man than that boar's tit she was married to, but she was in for a shock when she found out what it's really like out there when they take the cover off and let you look in. When that ocean started climbing up her leg she'd be screaming her tonsils loose. He didn't like to think about it himself. Well, it couldn't be any worse than jumping into France in the dark with those jugheads down there waiting for you. But that was a long time back. Sport, that was a *long* time back.

But, hell, you had to look on the bright side. Think about Hughie-boy. He wasn't going to drown. It brought the lump right up there in your throat just thinking that Mama's precious made it up the ladder before he chopped it loose. And he only had to kill four people to do it. But we don't mind, do we, fellows?

He went up on deck. . . .

It was 5:10 p.m. when the sun was blotted out and the squall burst around them. Ingram clung to the pump and looked along the deck in the fury of spray and horizontal, wind-hurled rain. Mrs. Warriner and Bellew crouched in the lee of the deckhouse, seeking the little protection they could find. Mrs. Warriner's hair was plastered to her head and face, and Bellew's Mexican hat was long since gone, blown overboard in the first onslaught of the wind. The deckhouse hatch was closed, as well as the two where they'd been bailing, and he and Bellew had lifted the dinghy aboard and lashed it. There was nothing else you could do. Except pray, and keep pumping.

Now that they were inside it, where all directions were the same and visibility was cut to a few yards, perspective was gone and there was no way of telling which way it was moving or how far they were from the edge, but he believed from having watched it as it made up that the worst of it was passing to the northward of them—for what that was worth. It wasn't the wind itself he was afraid of; it was the sea, and that was the same all around them.

It was high, steep-sided, and confused, fighting the

groundswell running up from the south. *Orpheus* had too little freeboard now, and she was too heavy-bellied and sluggish to ride with the punch and escape any of the beating she was taking. She pitched, lurched over, and was swept from bow to stern by every breaking sea, wallowing helplessly like some huge but mortally wounded animal. She rolled down too far and hung, pinned there on her beam ends for long moments by the inertia of the water inside her, and Ingram winced, thinking of the stresses as the enormous weight of the keel pulled the other way to bring her back. He could hear the creak and groan of her timbers even above the shrieking of the wind and knew that all the while more of her fastenings were working loose and pulling out of rotten frames and planks below him. Swung around and crouched to protect his face from the stinging of the rain and spray, he continued to pump, wondering about the bed bolts of the engine. And the great keel bolts themselves . . .

But they continued to hold, and in another twenty minutes it began to subside. The sun broke through. The wind dropped and then died completely, and they were still afloat. At six p.m., with the sun low on the horizon, the sea had quit breaking aboard, and they were able to open the hatches to resume bailing. When Ingram looked down at the depth of water in the after cabin he knew there was very little chance she would live through the night.

It was 1:40 p.m., five minutes now since Warriner had suddenly sprung to his feet and run back on deck to take the wheel. *Saracen* was plowing steadily ahead, back on course—whatever it was. Rae Ingram stood beside the sink in the after cabin, crushing the last of the three codeine tablets between the spoons. The bottle containing the others was recapped and stowed in one of the drawers, ready in case she needed more. She dropped the powder into the glass, but it was the other problem she was thinking of. This idea of hers, she felt sure, would still work. Within a few minutes—with any luck at all—she might be in command of *Saracen* again. But what good was it if she couldn't find her way back to the other boat?

The 226 degrees her compass had been reading meant nothing now that he'd smashed it and there was no way to compare it with the steering compass. It could have been as much as twenty or thirty degrees from the actual course. So as far as knowing what their course had been from the other boat, she was little better off than she'd been at the beginning, and now they were at least twenty-five miles away. Somehow she had to find out what he was steering. But how? Try to get a look into the binnacle when she went up? No, that wouldn't work. It was covered, so you could see into it only from the helmsman's seat, and he would be instantly suspicious if she tried to work her way around behind him. He wouldn't let her, and it might even trigger him into another outburst, which would wreck her chances of success with this idea. She couldn't risk it. Getting control of the boat came first. Wait, she thought, beginning to see the solution. The sun. It was shining, and far enough down from the meridian now to cast a good shadow. It wouldn't be exact, but it would be a good approximation, probably near enough to bring her back within sight of the other boat.

Working rapidly now, she dropped sugar into the glass with the powder from the pulverized tablets, put in a few spoonfuls of water to start it dissolving, and squeezed in a whole lemon. Then she opened the door of the tiny electric refrigerator inset in the after bulkhead and took two ice cubes from the tray. She finished filling the glass with water and stirred until there was no trace of the powder left in the bottom and the glass itself was beaded with moisture from the cold. Warriner had been sitting there in the sun since nine this morning with nothing to drink; there wasn't much chance he could resist it—especially if she didn't offer it to him and was drinking from it herself. A little of it wouldn't hurt her.

She carried it up the ladder into the hot glare of sunlight on deck. Warriner looked up from the compass with watchful appraisal but appeared to relax when she sat down on the after edge of the deckhouse beside the mizzenmast, rather than coming down into the cockpit. He said nothing. She ignored him, looking aft as if hoping to see the other boat following them. She took a sip of the lemonade.

The sun was diagonally behind her, falling over her left shoulder, which meant their course was somewhere in the vicinity of southwest. There was a good chance he was steering for the Marquesas or for Tahiti, but she couldn't depend on that because there was no guarantee he even knew the correct course to either of them. She had to narrow it down. Moodily, as if lost in thought, she let her gaze run idly along the scupper on the port quarter, the extreme edge of the deck where it was crossed by the shadow of the mizzenmast.

Of course the shadow was by no means stationary. With *Saracen*'s corkscrew motion as she quartered across the swell, and his deviations on either side of the course he was steering, it moved forward and aft along the edge of the deck as much as two feet or more. But by catching it several times when the boat was on an even keel to cancel out the rolling, she was able to strike an average between the extremes of his steering. The after edge of the shadow would be about three inches forward of that lifeline stanchion, and second one counting from astern. All she had to do, if and when she got the wheel, would be to line the shadow up on that spot, note the heading on the compass, and figure out the reciprocal. But was he going to take the bait? It had already been several minutes.

She looked aft and, without appearing even to notice him, saw that his eyes had been on the glass. She raised it to her mouth, took another sip, and set it beside her on the deckhouse while she reached in her pocket for a cigarette. It was well beaded with moisture, and she knew he could see the ice. How much longer could he stand it?

"What's that you're drinking?" he asked then.

"Lemonade," she said.

"Oh."

She put the cigarette in her mouth, and returned the pack to her pocket. Let him wait. Make him ask for it. Then she saw him look at the glass again and knew she had won. Her only problem had been to make him want it.

There was no way she could lose now, whether he suspected anything or not. If he asked her to bring him a glass, she would merely make another with three of the tablets in it. And whether he did or did not demand to trade after she'd given it to him, it made no difference. But she had an idea he would take the simple way. He did.

"It looks good," he said.

"Would you like me to make you one?" she asked.

There was a trace of slyness in his eyes now. Mother was all right when he was scared and needed her, but she wasn't going to put anything over on him. He was too smart for that. "Why not give me that one and make another for yourself?"

"But I've already drunk out of it," she protested.

"That doesn't matter." He smiled, as if thinking of some secret joke, and held out his hand.

She shrugged and handed it to him and started down the ladder. Then she turned and asked, "Would you like me to make you another while I'm at it?"

"No, this will do," he replied, still smiling. "And thanks a lot."

Once out of sight at the foot of the ladder, she hurried forward. That should have dispelled the last doubt, she thought, and he'd gulp it right down. How long would it take? Not more than five to ten minutes, probably, but with the first wave of drowsiness he was going to know she'd tricked him and he'd be dangerous until he finally collapsed. She'd better stay here, ready to barricade the door if she saw him start down the ladder, though she didn't believe he'd ever make it this far. Of course there was the chance he might think to close and fasten the hatch to lock her below, but it couldn't be helped. She didn't dare remain on deck. Anyway, noise would never wake him, that thoroughly drugged, and she could tear the hatch cover apart with a hammer and marlinspike and force her way out.

She grabbed a coiled heaving line, which was soft and easy to handle, and the knife she'd used to cut open the box of shotgun shells. With the door just cracked, she peered out, watching the hatch. A minute went by. Three. Ten. *Saracen* continued to plow ahead, apparently still on course. Had he become suspicious of it after all? She was sure there'd been no taste; it was well covered by the lemon and sugar. Then she felt *Saracen* lurch and begin to turn. At the same time a demonic cry shot up above the noise of the engine, like a prolonged scream of rage, and the glass came flying in the open hatch. It narrowly missed the radio and smashed against the bulkhead at the forward end of her bunk. *Saracen* rolled down and turned in the opposite direction. She continued to watch the hatch with apprehension, but sunlight fell through it unobstructed. Almost a full minute went by. Nothing happened except that *Saracen* continued to turn, as if she were going around in a tight circle. She could visualize what had happened. Trying to get up, holding onto the wheel, he'd turned it, and then collapsed across it.

She ran through the after cabin, mounted the first step of the ladder, and peered out. Then she froze. He had fallen forward across the wheel, but now he was moving again, making one last effort to get up. His face was distorted, and he cried out as though in rage against the darkness swimming up around him. One hand reached down to the engine control panel. The noise of the engine cut off abruptly, his arm swung, and she saw the ignition key flash in the sunlight as he threw it overboard.

The brass cover of the binnacle followed it over the side, and then, still screaming, he had hold of the compass itself, swinging in its gimbals. Muscles writhed in his arms and shoulders, and the tendons stood out in his throat. It tore free, and while he was turning with it in his hands to throw it into the sea he fell back onto the seat and collapsed with his head and shoulders on the narrow strip of deck beside him. The compass dropped on deck, burst with an eruption of alcohol, and slid over the side as *Saracen* rolled down to starboard. In the abrupt and almost terrifyingly lonely silence as *Saracen* slowed and came to rest she could only cling to the handrail of the ladder in defeat, and for a moment she wished she had killed him when she'd had the chance. There was no other compass aboard.

Then it was gone, and she was moving ahead. After

what she'd been through to get this far, nothing was going to stop her. She had no idea how she was going to find her way back across all those miles of open sea with nothing to guide her, but that would have to wait till she could get to it. The first thing was to tie him. Why, she wasn't quite sure, because he'd probably be unconscious for at least eight or ten hours and if she hadn't found the other boat in five or less she'd never find it at all and after that nothing mattered anyway, but he had to be immobilized once and for all. Maybe it had something to do with having been completely at his mercy for all those years since early this morning, and if there had been any way to embed him in a barrel of hardening concrete up to his neck she would have done it. She stood above him in the cockpit with her heaving line and her knife.

He hadn't moved since he'd fallen. She reached down to touch him, a little fearfully, and then realized nothing was going to rouse him now. He was still behind the wheel, and there was no possibility at all of moving him. He must weigh 180 or 190 pounds, and, inert as he was, it would take a professional weight-lifter to get him out of there. But it didn't matter. She could handle the wheel from the port seat of the cockpit, or standing up. The only thing that did matter was that she had to hurry.

She cut a piece about twelve feet long from the heaving line and bound his wrists together in front of him, going around them and then between them to form an unslippable pair of handcuffs. She stretched his arms out along the strip of deck and made the end of the line fast to a lifeline stanchion. Then she tied his ankles together and anchored them to the base of the binnacle. There was no way he could move at all. His face rested on his outstretched arms.

She stood up, wiped sweat from her face, and looked at her watch. It was 2:20 p.m. Her mind was instantly swamped with all the problems clamoring for attention, calculations of time and distance and the unknown factor of direction and the need to do everything at once, but she brushed them aside. One thing at a time, and the next was to start the engine. She couldn't stand the silence. Normally she disliked the noise as much as John did, but now she needed the comfort of it to be able to think. *Saracen* had come to rest and was rolling forlornly on the groundswell, completely becalmed and helpless on a sea as unruffled as glass and achingly empty in all directions to the far rim of the visible world, where it met the converging bowl of the sky. With John there, it was privacy, but now it was a loneliness that screamed.

She knelt and reached in under the engine-control panel. There were wires coming up to the ammeter as well as to the ignition switch, but she could identify them by location. There were only two to the switch. She twisted and yanked until she had broken them loose. She pulled them down into view and peeled the insulation from them with the knife; then she twisted the ends together, pulled the lever back to neutral, and pressed the starter button. The engine rumbled into life and began to roar. She eased the throttle back to idle.

Now . . .

All she had was the sun, and she'd only have that for another four hours—unless it disappeared before then before a cloudbank or in a squall. She'd been facing directly aft, and it had come diagonally over her left shoulder, so facing forward she'd want it in the same place. It wasn't much, she thought fearfully. But wait—she could do better than that.

What about the shadow of the mizzenmast, and her mark? If she projected the mark to the opposite side of the boat along the same plane she should be very near the reciprocal of the course he'd been steering. She grabbed up what was left of the heaving line, whirled, and caught the wire lifeline on the port quarter beside the cockpit. Three inches forward of the second stanchion, counting from aft. Right here. She made the end of the line fast, passed it ahead of the mizzen, and went up the starboard side with it. She pulled it taut, and then moved her end aft until it just touched the forward side of the mast. It intersected the starboard lifeline nearly midway between the third and fourth stanchions, again counting from aft. She tied it there, winding the surplus line three or four times around the wire to make it easier to see from the wheel.

At best it was still only a prayer, a stab in the dark. The bearing of the sun was going to change as it moved down toward the horizon, and there was no guarantee at all that Warriner had even gone back to his original course when he'd returned to the deck after smashing her compass. But, she thought, trying to still the fear inside her, all she had to do was come within four miles of *Orpheus* and she'd be able to see her.

She jumped back into the cockpit, pushed the lever into gear, ran the throttle up to about where Warriner had had it, and put the wheel over. Sitting on the port seat of the cockpit beside it, she could see her marker all right. She brought *Saracen* on around until the shadow of the mizzenmast fell on it, swinging back and forth on either side of it as she rolled. As she steadied up, she looked at her watch. It was 2:35 p.m.

How far, how many hours? It was a few minutes past two when Warriner had stopped the engine and thrown the key overboard. From nine this morning, that would be five hours since they'd left *Orpheus*—less the time he'd been below while *Saracen* was running God knew where with no one at the wheel. Call it four and a half hours—twenty-five to twenty-seven miles. At the same speed going back, she should be in the area at seven p.m. That would be a little after sunset, perhaps not quite dark, but by then she would be running blind.

So *Orpheus* had to be in sight by then, because there would be no second chance. If she weren't there, she'd already sunk, or the course had been wrong, and with no compass the latter was as irreversible as the first. Within a half-hour she'd be hopelessly lost herself, with no idea where she was going or where she'd been. She couldn't think about it. She tried to force everything from her mind but the mechanics of steering by the shadow of the mizzenmast and the continuing prayer that the sun would go on shining.

At a little after three she began to see the dark cloud in the north. The squall was still far over the horizon, but she couldn't take a chance of running into it with all sail set; they might be knocked down or dismasted. But she hated to stop, even for a few minutes. It appeared to be moving to the westward at the same time it was coming nearer; maybe it would be gone by the time she got there. But she should take in sail anyway; the main and the jib were going to interfere too much with her view ahead. At a little after four, while the sun was momentarily obscured by a passing cloud, she stopped and took in everything. She was under way again in less than twenty minutes, with the sun visible once more on the thinning edge of the cloud.

Warriner had never moved since he'd fallen. She began to be afraid the three tablets had been too much and she'd killed him. She reached over and touched his throat, and she could feel the pulse. It was slow but steady.

At four-thirty she reached inside the hatch for the binoculars and began to search the horizon to port and then to starboard between corrections to the helm. There was the chance *Orpheus* had got a breeze and John had tried to follow them. Her eyes encountered nothing but the empty miles of water and the far rim of that circle in which they seemed to be forever centered. The noise of the engine went on, they rose and fell in a long pitching motion as the glassy billows of the swell rolled up under her quarter, but they never appeared to move at all.

It was five o'clock. Five-thirty. The squall ahead was moving into the west and breaking up. Scattered clouds began to obscure the sun at intervals, but she went on, looking over her shoulder and trying to judge its position. She continued to search the horizon to port and starboard with the glasses. The sea was empty all around her. By six the tightness in her chest was becoming almost unbearable.

Six-thirty. The sun came out from behind another cloud, and it was far down now, less than a diameter above the horizon and beginning to redden in the haze. The shadow of the mizzenmast was gone. She stood up, holding the wheel with her right hand and steering with the sun just behind her left shoulder while she held the binoculars to her eyes and scanned the sea ahead.

The colors began. Far overhead the fleecy edges of clouds were touched with gold and then pink, darkening to crimson. The sun slid downward into the low cloudbank on the horizon, and in a moment it was gone from sight and there were only the vertical rays of pale lemon extending upward against the sky. Just for an instant the defenses of her mind gave way and she remembered sunsets she had watched with John here in this cockpit in the Bahamas and Caribbean and the Gulf of Panama. She began to tremble. She dropped the engine out of gear, pulled the throttle back to idle, and leaped up on deck. She climbed atop the main boom with an arm about the mast and slowly swung the binoculars all the way around from the already darkening east to the great flame of the afterglow in the west, and there was no sign of *Orpheus* anywhere. It was 7:05 p.m.

[15]

INGRAM'S EYES WERE BLEAK AS HE LOOKED DOWN INTO THE fading light of the main cabin. If you had any talent for kidding yourself, he thought, now would be a good time to break it out. With the two of them bailing and Mrs. Warriner at the pump, the water had gained several inches in the past half-hour. They must have lost whole planks off her outer skin in that squall.

He turned and searched the emptiness of the sea down to the southwest and then glanced at his watch. It was 6:50. He dropped the bucket on the deck and went back to the others. "Knock off a minute."

Bellew looked at him inquiringly. Mrs. Warriner straightened and pushed damp hair back from a face deeply lined with fatigue. "You mean we're gaining on it?"

He shook his head. "No. We're not even keeping up with it. But a quarter of an hour one way or the other's not going to make any difference, and before it gets too dark to see I want to have one more look around from the masthead."

He slung the glasses around his neck and shackled the sling to the main halyard again. He climbed atop the boom and stepped into the sling with his lifeline around the mast. "Haul away," he ordered. In the confused sea left behind by the squall, *Orpheus* was wallowing even worse than before, but he managed the tricky business of getting past the spreaders without accident. When he was up just short of the masthead light, he called down, "That'll do. Make fast."

They were lying on a southerly heading at the moment. Legs locked against the dizzying swing of the mast, he looked around him. In the east the blue was already beginning to darken with the coming of night, while off to starboard the sun had dropped over the horizon and the western sky was aflame. It was impossible to escape entirely the beauty of it or to seal the mind against all of memory's infiltration, and he was glad he was up here where they couldn't see his face. Then he put the glasses to his eyes and began a cold and methodical search of the horizon to the southwest, fighting the lunging of the mast. He moved on into the south, and around to the east, where the light was beginning to fade. Nothing. Still nothing . . .

Where was she now? Was she still alive? The glasses began to shake. He lowered them and closed his eyes. The feeling passed in a moment, and he had control of himself again. He raised the glasses and came back, very slowly, across the whole area he had searched before, and then on into the dying fire and the wine-red sea of the west. He stopped abruptly. Something came up into his throat, and he swallowed. He tried to swing the glasses back, but for an instant he couldn't. He was afraid to look again.

All right, he thought savagely; maybe you should have sent one of the men. He brought them back.

It was a mast.

Or was it? *Orpheus* rolled, and in the sickening swing out to port and back he lost the spot again. He got the line of the horizon in the glasses once more and inched to the right. There! It was only a tiny pencil stroke seen for an instant against the red glow of sunset. He locked his arms more tightly around the mast in an effort to stop the tremor of the glasses. It came into view, and this time he was certain he saw the other one beside it, the two of them like the tips of two toothpicks held at arm's length before a fire. The shorter one was to the left.

"Lower away!" he shouted.

He knew what they had to do and made up his mind as he came down the mast. Below him, the others looked up silently, their faces almost red in the winy light. He landed on the boom, stepped out of the sling, and jumped down beside them.

"She's over there," he began. When they started to interrupt, he cut them off with a curt gesture. "Wait till I get through. She's going to miss us. She's hull down, even from up there; all I got was a glimpse of the masts against the sunset. She's due west of us, headed north, and she won't get any closer. From where she is, down on deck, we're clear over the horizon, so there's no way in God's world she can see us—"

"There's no way we can signal her?" Mrs. Warriner asked.

"Just one. Set this one afire."

"Oh." She gave him a startled look, and then she was calm again. "Could she see it from over there?"

"I think so."

"You *think* so?" Bellew interrupted. "That's great."

"Shut up." He went on. "There's a good chance. We're to the east of her, so it'll be dark behind us in another fifteen minutes. And there are enough clouds overhead to reflect the glow."

"And if she doesn't see us?" Bellew asked. "But don't bother to tell me, let me guess. We take a taxi to the McAlpin Hotel—"

"We do the same thing we're going to do anyway," Ingram said coldly. "We drown. The water's gained at least three inches on us in the past half-hour, with all three of us working. She won't last till midnight." They were wasting time with this idiotic argument. He swung around to

Mrs. Warriner. "It's your yacht, and you're still aboard it—"

"Burn it, of course," she said coolly.

Bellew shrugged. "Okay. What are we waiting for?"

"Will it burn?" she asked. "I mean, this low in the water, and with everything up here wet from the squall?"

"We'll fire it in the chartroom," Ingram replied. "There's no gasoline left at all?"

"No."

"What does your galley stove burn? Bottled gas, or kerosene?"

"Kerosene. There should be several cans of it in the locker forward."

"Right. What about paint stores—turpentine, linseed oil, thinner?"

"There should be some of each."

"Good." He began to issue terse orders. "Get your passports, money, and the logbook; you can't take anything else. Wrap them in something waterproof. Dump the water out of that dinghy and stow 'em in there, along with a couple of flashlights. Put on lifebelts, and then you can give me a hand."

Without even waiting for a reply, he whirled and ran down into the chartroom. He grabbed a flashlight from its bracket and went on down the steps and through the main and forward cabins, where the debris-laden water washed around his thighs. Opposite the sail bin was another locker. He unlatched the doors and yanked them open but could see nothing in the thickening gloom here below. He switched on the flashlight and wedged it between two of the sailbags. In an upper compartment were some tools and paint brushes. He spied a small hand ax and stuck the handle of it in his belt. The bottom of the locker was filled with buckets and rectangular one-gallon cans submerged and bumping together in the water that surged back and forth.

The buckets would be paint. He ignored them and began fishing out the cans. There were a dozen of them, mostly unidentifiable, the labels long since washed off, but it didn't matter. An armful at a time, he carried them up the ladder going on deck from the forward cabin and dumped them beside the hatch. As he made the last trip he saw that Bellew and Mrs. Warriner had returned to the deck, wearing lifebelts, and Bellew had the dinghy up on its side, pouring the water out of it.

The great flame in the west was dying now, and the brief twilight of the tropics had already begun. He grabbed up two of the cans and ran aft.

"What now?" Bellew asked.

"Let's get the dinghy over." With a swing of the hand ax he knocked out one of the windows of the deckhouse and tossed the two cans in on the chartroom table. Mrs. Warriner was holding two flashlights and a package wrapped in oilskins. As she stowed them in the dinghy he noticed the compass had fallen out when Bellew had dumped out the water. It wasn't broken. He put it back in.

"Grab the bow," he said to Bellew. They lifted it over the lifeline and, when *Orpheus* rolled down, set it in the water. It rode lightly on the heavy swell passing beneath them. He handed the painter to Mrs. Warriner. "Take it aft and just wait. Keep it fended off so it doesn't get caught under the counter."

Whirling to Bellew, he said, "Bring up a couple of those spare sails from the locker. It doesn't matter which ones. Dump 'em there alongside the mainmast. And then bring all those cans aft, the ones around the forward hatch."

"Where do you want 'em?" Bellew asked.

"Just forward of the cockpit's all right." He turned and ran down the steps into the chartroom. Quick blows of the hand ax knocked out the rest of the windows. He began yanking drawers out of the chart table and smashing them with the ax after he had dumped out the charts. He tore charts into strips until he had a great armful of paper. He piled this on a corner of the table and threw the splintered drawers on top of it. With another blow of the ax he cut through one of the cans. As the liquid gushed out, he could tell by the smell of it that it was paint-thinner. He poured it over the paper and wood and cut open the other can. This one was kerosene. He swung it, splashing the bulkheads, the deck, and the table. Grabbing up another chart, he flicked his cigar lighter. The lighter was wet and required several attempts before it worked. He held it to the corner of the chart and, when it was burning, tossed it on the pile. With a great sucking sound it all burst into flame at once. He threw the rest of the charts on it and ran out.

Bellew had the two sailbags piled beside the mainmast now and was hurrying back and forth, carrying the cans aft. With his knife open, beginning at the end of the boom, Ingram went forward, slicing through the gaskets of the furled mainsail. When he reached the mast he unshackled the sling and made the halyard fast to the head of the sail again. Two more quick slashes split the sailbags. He hauled the sails out and stretched them along the deck, one atop the other. He grabbed up a line at random, cut off a length, made it fast around the two sails somewhere near the center, and hauled the whole cumbersome bundle over to the base of the mast. He made the line fast to the halyard above the shackle.

Bellew was passing then with the last of the cans. He grabbed two of them from his arms and swung the ax on them. The first was linseed oil. He poured it on the two sails. The other was kerosene. He dumped this on them also, and onto the mainsail, which was dangling in folds along the boom. He could hear the fire beginning to roar below him now, and smoke was pouring through the broken windows. "Give me a hand on this halyard," he called out to Bellew.

They hoisted. The mainsail went up, and with it the great dangling mass of the two spare sails made fast to the head of it. Kerosene and linseed oil began to drip on them.

Bellew grunted. "For that real homey feeling, it ought to be gasoline."

"If it breaks out of the chartroom," Ingram said, "go right over the side."

"Don't give it a thought, sport. I just look stupid."

It was up. Ingram threw the hitches on the pin, and they ran aft. Flame was beginning to lick through the broken windows. "Into the dinghy," he ordered and nodded to

Bellew. "You first. Take the oars." Bellew stepped down into it and held it while he helped Mrs. Warriner in.

She protested. "Aren't you going to get in?"

"It won't take three; it'll capsize."

"But you haven't even got a lifebelt—"

He cut her off. "I don't need one. Pull clear and wait for me. I want this thing to go all at once, and go high—the higher the better. Get going." He waved them off. Bellew shipped the oars and they began to draw away in the thickening dusk, heaving up and down on the swell.

There were eight of the rectangular cans on deck at the forward end of the cockpit. He set them up on end one at a time and began swinging the ax. The first was spar varnish. He picked it up and threw it forward. It landed just beyond the mainmast and slid, spilling its contents along the deck. The next was kerosene. It went up the other side of the deck. Turpentine. It followed the varnish. Paint-thinner. That was the trigger, the most volatile of them all. He set it aside, upright on the cockpit seat with his knee braced against it so it wouldn't turn over and spill. Linseed oil. He threw it forward. It bounced and slid, spraying along the deck. The whole interior of the chartroom was a roaring mass of flame now, and he could feel the heat on his face. The varnish on the underside of the main boom was beginning to bubble. He had to hurry. There were only seconds left before it broke out through the roof.

He swung the ax on another can, and another. Some of them had already slid overboard, but their contents had spilled, and the whole deck forward of him was criss-crossed with trails of varnish, linseed oil, turpentine, and kerosene, flowing across the planks and soaking into the seams. The final can was another of paint-thinner. He dropped the ax and picked it up, along with the other can, the one beside his knee.

He ran to the after end of the cockpit and jumped up onto the narrow strip of deck right on the stern. *All right, honey, this is where we are.* Wheeling, he threw the first can straight through a window into the inferno inside the chartroom, and while it was still in the air he threw the other and dived over the side.

Thirty yards away in the gathering night, Lillian Warriner turned and stared in wonder. My God, she thought, they shouldn't match him against just one ocean at a time. Even while his body was still in the air, a great ball of flame burst out of the chartroom, taking the roof of the deckhouse with it and igniting the whole ketch forward of the cockpit in one mighty breath. Fire shot up the oil-soaked mainsail and ballooned in the two sails at the top of it to form—with the force of the explosion and the massive updraft from the heat below—a gigantic torch, a column of flame nearly a hundred feet high. It lit up the sea for a quarter-mile in every direction, and she could feel the heat of it on her skin.

Then he was alongside, with a hand on the gunwale. He dropped his sneakers into the dinghy. They rose as a swell passed under them. "You haven't got much freeboard," he said, "but I think it'll ride if you don't make any sudden moves. If it does swamp, the flashlights are more important than your passports and money. Try to keep at least one of them out of the water. There's no use staying here; keep rowing west."

Bellew turned his head, trying to see the dying band of color along the western horizon. "I'm blind," he said, "with that glare in my face."

"Set the compass between your feet," Ingram said to Mrs. Warriner. "Line it up with the bow, and hold a flashlight on it so he can see it."

She did. Bellew began to pull slowly ahead. Ingram held onto the transom very lightly with one hand and kicked with his feet. When they were a hundred yards away he turned and looked back. It was like a scene from hell, he thought, with the red glare reflected on the black and oily heaving of the sea. The first great pillar of flame had died now that the sails were gone, and they were already in the edge of the surrounding darkness, but she was burning fiercely from bow to stern. The glow in the sky would still be visible for miles.

"Will it last long enough for her to get here?" Mrs. Warriner asked above him.

"No," he said. "It'll burn to the waterline and sink in twenty minutes or so. It'll take her an hour, or an hour and a half. But it doesn't matter; she'll take a bearing on it and have a compass course."

She made no reply. They went on toward the darkness. He thought she might turn for one last look, but she didn't. She remained quite still, her face lowered over the compass between her feet. It was possible she was crying, but if she was, he thought, nobody would ever know it except her.

The same question was in both their minds, he knew, the same dread of what they might find aboard *Saracen*. He thought of the shotgun and shivered.

She'd got under way again because she had to keep moving as long as she could. The silence was out there waiting for her, and once she stopped and killed the engine with the acceptance of final defeat she would be defenseless and she wasn't sure she would survive it.

It was 7:20 p.m. There was still enough faint light and dying color along the rim of the horizon to show her where west was, and there would continue to be, probably, for another ten minutes. Everywhere else it was already night. Across from her, Warriner's naked shoulders and golden head were only a faint gleam in the darkness. She was standing up, holding the wheel with one hand and staring ahead into the north, when something flickered on the extreme edge of her peripheral vision. She turned her head and saw the little tongue of reddish light lick upward over the edge of the world far off to the eastward.

For a second or two she could only stare at it in a sort of stunned disbelief. Then tears came up into her eyes and blinded her for an instant as this gave way to a great surge of joy, but by then she already had the wheel hard over and was coming around. She lined it up alongside the masts and reached for the throttle. The engine noise increased to a roar as it came up the final notch to full wide open.

How far? She'd seen nothing there before, even with the binoculars, which meant it was clear over the horizon—six, eight, or even ten miles away. But John must have seen her against the sunset and then deliberately set *Orpheus* afire because he had no other way to signal her. The only way he could have seen her would have been from the masthead, so there were probably others aboard. But that was unimportant at the moment. She had something to guide her now. That was all that mattered.

In another few minutes the little tip of flame was no longer showing over the horizon, but the glow was clearly visible against the sky. She felt a moment's uneasiness. How long would it burn before it sank? If it were even eight miles away, it would take her nearly an hour and a half to get there. It was almost due east, but that was no help once the last of the light was gone from the west and all directions were the same. She had to have a star or some constellation she could recognize, one still low enough on the horizon to give her the direction. But ahead of her, above the glow, the sky was becoming overcast. Almost instinctively she glanced to the north before she remembered Polaris was below the horizon now. They were south of the equator.

She turned to look astern, and saw the answer, if the sky remained clear enough in the west. Venus had just emerged from behind a cloud. It was perhaps three hours behind the sun, well down toward the horizon directly behind her. She faced forward, less worried now. Twenty minutes passed. The faint reddish glow was still visible ahead, reflected from the underside of the clouds above it. She kept it lined up beside the masts. It began to fade. Then, thirty-five minutes after she had first sighted it, it disappeared with the abruptness of a snuffed-out candle. *Orpheus* had gone down.

Venus was still bright behind her. She went on. It was awkward and not very accurate, trying to steer looking over her shoulder, so she stood up, facing aft directly before the wheel, and tried to keep the planet poised over the end of the mizzen boom. She reached inside the hatch and switched on the running lights. Venus began to disappear in the edge of another cloud. She tried to guess its bearing, but when it reappeared fifteen minutes later it was far around to starboard. She'd been running almost south.

She swung the wheel to bring it astern again and turned herself, to look forward, searching the horizon on both sides and ahead for any tiny pinpoint of light. She must be within two or three miles of them. On all sides the darkness was unbroken. Then Venus faded and disappeared again. The western sky was becoming overcast. Directly overhead stars were visible through holes in the clouds but there was nothing anywhere that was low enough on the horizon to guide her. In two more minutes she was hopelessly lost, with no more knowledge of direction than if she were at the bottom of a well.

She jerked the throttle back and threw the engine out of gear. It was absolutely imperative now that she stay exactly where she was; every turn of the propeller could be taking her away from them instead of nearer. She pulled the twisted wires apart to stop the engine's roar so she could listen as she climbed atop the main boom to search the darkness all around. There was no light, no cry. She came down from the boom and ran below for a can of flares.

There was no fire behind them now; *Orpheus* had gone down nearly fifteen minutes ago. "Still nothing," Mrs. Warriner said above him in the darkness. Each time they crested a swell she searched the sea ahead, while Bellew continued to pull at the oars.

"What time is it now?" he asked.

She held her watch under the beam of the flashlight. "Eight-ten."

It had been fifty minutes. They should have picked up *Saracen*'s masthead light by now. "You've got too much light under you," he said. "Hold the flashlight by the lens so it's completely covered by your hand except one spot right over the compass. Bellew will still be able to see it. Then put that bundle of oilskins across your lap so no light seeps up at all. And when you locate the horizon, don't look directly at it; look a little above. Night vision's better out of the edges of your eyes."

Down in the water behind the dinghy, he could see nothing at all. Another fifteen minutes went by. The dark undulations of the swell rolled up under them and slid past in silence except for the creak of oarlocks. "Maybe if I stood up——" she said.

"No. You'll capsize. We're bound to pick her up in a minute. We're still right on course? Bellew, I mean; don't look down at the light yourself."

"Due west all the time," Bellew replied. Then he went on, an undertone of ugliness in his voice. "You know what, sport? Wouldn't it be a real gas if you didn't see any masts over there?"

"I saw masts," Ingram said coldly. It was for Mrs. Warriner's benefit. He had no interest at all in what Bellew thought.

There was a sudden cry from Mrs. Warriner. "I see her! I see her!"

"Where?"

"Way off to the left. My left."

"All right," he said calmly. "Don't take your eyes off it. Bellew, pull your left oar till she tells you to steady up, and then check your compass."

Bellew came around. "Steady. Right there," Mrs. Warriner said.

"Almost due south," Bellew reported. "One-eighty-five to one-ninety."

Ingram swam out from behind the dinghy, and when they rose to the next swell peered into the darkness ahead. He could see nothing at all. He was too low. But why was she so far off course? At a distance of even eight miles she should have passed within a few hundred yards of them. "Can you see the port running light?" he asked.

"No. Only the masthead light," Mrs. Warriner replied. "She must be a mile, or two miles away. Wait. I think I saw the red light then. Yes, there it is. She must have been going away from us, and then turned."

"All right," he said. "Forget the compass for a minute. You can keep Bellew headed straight. Take both your flashlights and hold 'em as far over your head as you can——"

He was interrupted by a sudden cry from Mrs. Warriner, and at the same instant he saw it himself. A rocket arched into the sky ahead of them, hung poised for an instant, and began to float down like some great glowing flower.

"She's lost herself," Bellew said. "Hell, I thought you said she could take a bearing—"

Ingram cut him off savagely. "Save it!" Then he went on to Mrs. Warriner. "As soon as that goes out and she can see again, start waving your lights, pointed straight at her."

She held them ready but made no reply, and he wondered if she were prey to the same chilling thoughts that were running through his own mind. Probably. Anybody but a stupid meathead like Bellew would know something must be wrong aboard *Saracen*. Was she hurt? Or had she killed Warriner and now was beginning to go to pieces? Then the flare went out ahead of them, and Mrs. Warriner was signaling. Several minutes went by while they rose and fell in silence.

Then Mrs. Warriner cried out. "She's turned. I can see both running lights!"

Ingram sighed. She'd sighted them and was coming.

[16]

THE RANGE WAS CLOSING. AHEAD OF HER THE FLASHING lights were less than a quarter-mile away. Then it occurred to her he might be in the water instead of the dinghy, and she left the wheel long enough to run forward and hang the ladder over the side. Her knees were suddenly too weak to support her, and she almost fell coming back to the cockpit. It was difficult to breathe, and she was conscious of the pounding of her heart. She stared ahead at the two flashlights as if trying to burn away the darkness surrounding them. Two hundred yards . . .

She brought the throttle back and reached inside the hatch to turn on the spreader lights. The sea was illuminated for twenty or thirty yards on all sides of her, but she could still see the signals dead ahead.

She came hard left, and then right. She pulled the lever into reverse and backed down, racing the engine. *Saracen* came to rest, and the lights were less than fifty yards away, directly abeam. She reached down and yanked the wires apart, and in a sudden silence she could hear the rattle of oarlocks. He was in the dinghy. She leaned across the cockpit seat, staring outward.

Now she could see it. It was coming into the outer limits of the spreader lights. There were two people in it. John was rowing, and there was somebody smaller in the stern. She thought it was a woman— It wasn't John rowing. He was bigger than John. It was somebody she'd never seen before, and the other one was a woman, and there was nobody else. Then she saw the head come out from behind the dinghy, the man swimming, and the upraised arm waving to her. She slid down into the cockpit seat with one hand still feebly clutching the lifeline above her, unable even to raise her head, and her diaphragm began to kick so she couldn't exhale. Everytime she would try to breathe out, it would kick and she would inhale again.

Ingram saw her slide down and could see no sign of Warriner. "I'll go aboard first," he said to Mrs. Warriner. She was staring straight ahead, and when *Saracen* rolled down she thought she saw something on the other side of the cockpit, beyond Mrs. Ingram. Something sprawled. "Yes," she said in a controlled but very fragile voice. "Yes. Thank you."

Ingram lunged ahead and went up the ladder while they were coming alongside. Rae was sitting up now, and was apparently unhurt except for that bruise on her face. Beyond her he could see Warriner's body, but in the same glance he saw the bound wrists and the line going forward to the stanchion, and all the breath went out of him at once.

Rae was still looking up at him. "He smash—he smu—he smu—" She tried to point, but he had already seen the uncovered and empty binnacle, like an eyeless socket, and understood. Probably wrecked the other one too, he thought. So she came all the way back and found us with nothing at all. He wanted to say something, but his eyes had begun to sting, and he didn't trust his voice. Without even looking around, he gestured for the others to come aboard and reached down for her arm. She made it to her feet. She went down the ladder, and when she was in the darkness at the bottom of it, she turned.

She still couldn't say anything. She couldn't even cry. She was wrung out, drained, emptied of everything. She could only manage to get her arms up around his neck and cling while his went on crushing her, moving up and down her back as if they couldn't find any place they wanted to stay, while water dripped on her and whiskers ground into her face and the voice was saying, "Oh, Jesus Christ—oh, Jesus Christ—" against her throat.

The last handhold crumbled then, but instead of falling she was floating upward into some welcoming and completely sheltered oblivion, like a child's going to sleep. She felt herself being lifted and placed on the bunk. The arms still bound her, and the voice went on with its profane and ragged whispering, this time into her hair. Then, just before she disappeared entirely into the mist, she heard her own voice say something at last.

"Did you have any lunch?" she asked.

"No," he said. He swallowed and rubbed a hand across his eyes. "I guess I forgot." He kissed her again but knew she was gone. He still knelt beside her, and now he brought a hand up and placed the finger tips very gently against her throat to feel the pulse. And even after he was reassured she was all right, that she had merely reached the limit of endurance and stopped for a moment, he left the hand there, feeling her life run steadily on beneath his fingers. He didn't even know why he did it.

He got up for a cloth to bathe her face, and when he switched on the lights he saw the battered shotgun barrels on the deck beside the ladder. He took a long and shaky breath and shook his head.

She was just beginning to stir again when he heard the voices above him, the one a lashing impassioned whisper, *"Leave him alone!"* followed by the sharp slap of palm on flesh, and hoped she hadn't heard too. After what she'd been through, she deserved at least a few minutes of thinking it was all over. He thought of what was ahead of them and suddenly felt very old and tired. But the only chance they had was to meet it now, and head-on. He ran up the ladder.

Mrs. Warriner was trying to get up from where she was sprawled back on the cockpit seat. Beyond her, Bellew was standing on the narrow strip of deck, trying to turn Warriner's face up with the toe of his shoe. "Wake up, old Hughie-boy, and see who's here."

"All right, Bellew," he ordered, "leave him alone."

The other turned, and in the glow of the spreader lights above and forward of them he could see the insolence in the eyes. "Easy does it, Hotspur. You got your boat back, so just simmer down. This is mine."

"That's right; I got it back. And I give the orders on it. You heard what I said." There was no area for compromise here, not with Bellew. If it meant forcing the issue now, within the first five minutes, force it. But at that moment Mrs. Warriner sat up, the side of her face still red from the slap. Her voice was level and very cold as she spoke to Bellew. "I warn you. Don't touch him."

Bellew sat down on the opposite side of the cockpit. He leaned forward and tapped her on the knee with a forefinger. "Don't crowd me. I've had it. With you *and* your gold-plated fag."

Twelve hundred miles, Ingram thought, in a forty-foot yacht, with the third one crazy. He wondered what Lloyds would quote you on that. "That'll do," he snapped. He felt a little better now that Bellew had sat down. The situation wasn't going to explode as long as Warriner was asleep, or knocked out, or whatever he was. If he could leave the three of them alone for as long as five seconds he might find out.

"It does seem to me," Mrs. Warriner said then, "that one of us might make at least some casual inquiry as to how Mrs. Ingram is." She turned to him. "Is she hurt?"

"No," he said. "Not as far as I could tell. She's had a little too much for one day, and she fainted, but she's coming around now." He turned to go back below. It should be safe enough now, and Mrs. Warriner would sing out if anything happened.

"How'd she get the creep tied up?" Bellew asked.

"How the hell do I know?" he said. "I had some stupid idea that after a whole day of it I might get a chance to talk to her for a minute and a half——" He broke off, realizing he had to keep his temper.

"Sure, sure." Bellew grinned coldly. "I can understand you might have been a little worried. That's where I was one up on you, chum. I didn't have to worry about mine; I knew where she was."

That was the question you always had to ask yourself, Ingram thought, before you jumped all the way down his throat. Suppose it *had* been Rae? But it didn't change anything; it would be as stupid as hating the Pacific Ocean because she'd been swept overboard by a sea. "Bellew, for Christ's sake, don't you think I realize what it's like? But it's just something you can't change; you'll only make it worse——"

"What do you mean?" Mrs. Warriner interrupted.

She knows, he thought; she knows, all right, but she just won't accept it. At that moment Rae's head appeared above the hatch. So he wasn't even going to get a moment to talk to her alone, to fill her in on who these people were and what had to be done. In fact, for at least the next twenty to twenty-five days—assuming they lived that long —he'd never have a minute completely alone with her. He was conscious of a dark and futile anger but choked it off. The situation was still far too dangerous to be crying over lost privacy and interrupted honeymoons.

He sprang to help her and seated her on the after edge of the deckhouse. "Are you all right now, honey?"

She managed a smile. "Yes. Just a little weak from the reaction."

"Aren't we all?" He turned, indicating the others. "This is Mrs. Warriner. And Mr. Bellew."

"Hi," Bellew said. Mrs. Warriner leaned forward and took her hand, and said simply, "Thank you. And I'm sorry."

"It's all right," Rae said. "It's all over now——" She broke off and gasped. "John! The other compass! He smashed that too. We haven't got anything."

Ingram nodded. "I figured he had, or you'd have had it up here. But it's all right. There's one in the dinghy. I can make it do."

He stepped forward and lifted it out. The others had already removed the flashlights and the oilskin package containing their passports. He cast off the painter and pushed the dinghy away from the side. Holding the compass very carefully, he went below and stowed it in a drawer. It was beyond price now, and nothing was going to happen to it until he could get it secured in or on the binnacle. He still didn't know what was going to happen up there. He went back and sat down beside Rae. "All right, honey, if you're up to it now, can you tell us what happened? How did you get him tied up?"

"Codeine," she said. "I gave him three of those codeine tablets from the medicine chest, in a glass of lemonade. I think he's still all right, and it's been over six hours."

The others watched silently while he stepped over and reached down to check Warriner's pulse. He knew Mrs. Warriner would have already, but he wanted to be sure himself. It was steady. "He's okay," he said. He came back.

Rae told them the rest of the story. When she had finished, she looked at Mrs. Warriner. "I still don't know. I mean, if the codeine idea hadn't worked, and he hadn't smashed the shotgun."

Mrs. Warriner touched her on the arm. "I understand, dear. And you'll forget it eventually. We all just thank God it ended the way it did."

"Well, don't break up, girls," Bellew said. "Mama's precious is a-l-l right; he's not hurt. Tomorrow you can draw straws to see who's the lucky girl he'll kill next."

Rae shot a startled and puzzled glance at Ingram. "What happened to him? I couldn't make any sense of what he was saying. Something about a shark."

Before Ingram could reply, Mrs. Warriner and Bellew both spoke at once. Bellew overrode her. "Well, nothing much." He spread his hands in a deprecating gesture. "He killed my wife, and then this morning he slugged me and locked us in the cabin on there to drown when he abandoned ship. But, I mean, hell, nobody minds these little jokes as long as they keep Hughie happy—"

"He didn't kill your wife!" Mrs. Warriner lashed out. "And why don't you go ahead and tell the Ingrams why he locked us in there?"

"Wait a minute! Hold it!" Ingram cut them both off. "Rae's entitled to know what this is all about." As briefly as he could, he told her something of it.

Then he went on, to Mrs. Warriner and Bellew. "I want both of you to listen to me a minute. After your experience on *Orpheus* I shouldn't think you'd have too much trouble understanding what we're up against. We're twelve hundred miles from land, we still don't know when we'll pick up the Trades, and with the very best of luck it could be twenty days or more we're going to be jammed in here. There are five of us on a yacht with cruising accommodations for two, and one's unbalanced and dangerous and is going to have to be tied up and watched every minute to keep him from killing himself or somebody else—"

"Unh-unh," Bellew interrupted. "No sweat at all, pal. All he's going to need is a basket."

"So you're going to kill him? In front of three witnesses. Just what do you do then? Kill us too?"

"I'm not going to kill him. You think I'm stupid, or something? You might say I'm going to immobilize him—"

"Maybe you'd better wait till I get through," Ingram said. "You might change your mind. If you don't, there's a good chance none of us will ever reach land. We've got enough food, and the water will stretch, with rationing. But that's not it. I'm the only one on here that can take this boat down there—the only one who can navigate well enough, in the first place, and the only one who can compensate that compass so we won't be wandering all over hell and halfway back, trying to make a landfall. And I'm not going to stand here and just look on—any more than Mrs. Warriner is—while you make a cripple or a permanent imbecile out of a boy who's not responsible for his actions—"

"Jesus Christ, you too?"

"I said wait till I get through. To beat up a man in his mental condition, you'd have to be sicker than he is. And as I told you, none of us is going to stand here and watch it, so if you lay a hand on him this thing is going to blow wide open. I'd say there's a good chance you can whip me, but if I get beaten up so badly I can't sail this boat or navigate, you're not doing yourself any favor, unless you think you'd like drifting around out here while your tongue swells up and you go crazy.

"And there's another thing I don't think you've thought of. He's scared to death of you, and if you touch him he'll go completely berserk. You may be stupid enough to want to see what'll happen when a man runs amok on a forty-foot yacht with four other people on it, but the rest of us are not. Also, this is no hospital, so what do you do if he dies? So far, everything that's happened has been the result of an accident or bad luck or his crackup, and nobody's committed a deliberately criminal act—"

"You call what he did to my wife an accident?"

"For Christ's sake, Bellew, he panicked! You want to beat him to death because he got scared and lost his head?"

"Captain Ingram!" It was Mrs. Warriner this time. Well, he'd been expecting it.

He turned to her. "Bellew's right," he said wearily, "and you know it. I don't know why you want to saddle yourself with the blame for the whole thing, but your husband didn't crack up because he thought you and Bellew tried to kill him. That's just another place to hide, another way to try to pass the buck. There's no doubt he's afraid of Bellew, and he'll be ten times as afraid of him now, but nobody in his right mind who'd known you for as long as an hour would ever believe anything as stupid as that. He was already irrational when he came up with that gem—"

"Wait a minute!" Mrs. Warriner interrupted. "You still don't know the whole story. Why do you think we were both in that one cabin when you found us? Hughie hit Bellew and locked us in there because when he came below he found this vermin—this incredible, filthy, loathsome pig—already there trying to get into bed with me. What was he supposed to think? If he'd had any doubts before, that would settle them. I hadn't made any noise; being raped was preferable to having Hughie come running down there and probably be beaten to death."

Ingram looked at Bellew, trying to keep the contempt from showing any more than necessary. Don't push him, he thought; he's pretty close to the edge. But the latter was completely at ease. "Rape! Geez! So maybe I was trying to collect what you owed me; it had nothing to do with it, anyway. Hughie-boy already had his club with him when he came down there. He brought it from deck, because he'd already sighted this boat over here."

The son of a bitch, Ingram thought. The dirty, sad—

"If you were that broken up over your wife's death," Rae asked, "how did you ever happen to notice she was missing?"

Ingram gripped her arm and shook his head at her, but neither of the others had heard her anyway.

At least he knew now why Mrs. Warriner insisted on assuming all the guilt, even if she was probably still wrong. "Listen," he said, "that doesn't change anything. He locked you in there because he was already irrational, and he *was* irrational simply because his mind refused to accept the fact he'd been responsible for Mrs. Bellew's death." Then he wondered if he was being very smart. This would only inflame Bellew even more. No, Bellew already knew it anyway, and if he was brutal and stupid enough to want to smash up a boy who was mentally sick, this was merely superfluous and would have no effect on him one way or the other. And somehow he had to reach Mrs. Warriner.

Even while he was conscious of a faint self-disgust for

beginning to sound like a cocktail-party psychiatrist, he couldn't escape the feeling that her illogical burden of guilt was probably as dangerous here as Bellew's vindictiveness, and just as likely to trigger an explosion. And certainly it made it a lot more dangerous, and unnecessarily dangerous, for her. Not having any interest at all in what happened to her if anything happened to Warriner, she'd attack Bellew with anything in sight, and the consequences of that wouldn't be anything you'd ever want to remember —if you lived long enough to remember anything. Then, just for a moment, he was tempted to throw up his hands and let the three of them go ahead and kill themselves. Why did he have to defend Warriner, who'd caused the whole thing, when obviously his responsibility was to Rae? Was he going to endanger her life again for the alibi-artist, merely because he was helpless? But he knew he couldn't turn his back on it, even aside from the fact that once it started it couldn't be contained or avoided anyway. And, in the end, there was always Mrs. Warriner. She was worth fifty of the other two, and you couldn't let her throw herself into the meat-grinder from some misguided feeling of guilt.

"For God's sake," he went on wearily, "none of it was your fault, and you're not even doing him any good by trying to take the blame. I'm no head-shrinker, but it seems to me the chances are very good he can be brought out of it, with proper treatment. But he *has* to admit it. I don't think it's a feeling of guilt that made him crack up, but just the refusal to accept the blame. And as long as you go on grabbing all of it in sight, he never will. Jesus, there's no crime in losing your head. Anybody can do it; it's unpredictable. You know that yourself, Bellew—"

"No, I don't, good-buddy. I say nobody but a limp-wristed punk like Hughie-boy could do it, but then I'd never argue with a smart bastard like you. Why don't you write a book?"

He bit down hard on his temper. The whole attempt to appeal to the man had been futile, and any minute it was going to get out of hand. He had to move Warriner, and he'd better do it now, before he waked up. If he could get him shut up in that forward cabin, out of sight, they might make it through the night without an eruption of violence, and by morning Bellew would have had a chance to think twice about it. But getting him out from behind the wheel and down the ladder wasn't going to be easy. He was on the point of telling Bellew to give him a hand when he remembered the old axiom: never give an order you know is going to be ignored.

He turned to Mrs. Warriner. "I think the best place for him is in the forward cabin. The rest of us can use the two bunks in the main cabin in relays, or flake out on deck, subject to the watches we work out. So if you'll take his feet, we'll move him down there now."

"Yes, of course," she said. She stood up.

"No," Bellew said. "As you were."

"What?" she asked.

"Goldilocks stays right where he is." Bellew reached out a foot, put it against her midriff, and pushed. She sat down again.

There was no point in even saying anything, Ingram thought coldly. The act was deliberate and self-explanatory. He was already on his feet, and he hit Bellew as hard as he could just under the ear, as he was getting to his. The only chance he had was to hurt him, and hurt him badly, right at the start. But even as the blow landed, he knew he'd lost. Bellew rolled back with it with the ease and the beautiful reflexes of a pro and counterpunched with almost unbelievable speed for a man his size. Ingram felt the wind go out of him as a fist like a concrete block slammed into his stomach; and then another, which he only partially blocked, hit him over the heart. He started to fall but came back against the mizzen. Bellew hit him twice more in the stomach. Sickness ballooned inside him. He heard Rae shriek behind him, and Mrs. Warriner was trying to get past him to reach Bellew herself.

It was no place to fight; there was no room. He pushed off the mast, blocked Bellew's next punch, and managed to get under his guard with a right. *Saracen* rolled down to starboard. Bellew straightened, off balance, and Ingram hit him again. Bellew went back across the cockpit seat. Ingram swung again, lost his balance, and came down on top of him. They were in the after end of the cockpit, against the binnacle, and Ingram landed with his right forearm across the side of Warriner's face. Warriner stirred and groaned.

Ingram felt an arm lock around his neck and the thumb of the other hand groping for his eyes. He ducked his face down in Bellew's throat and brought his right hand up, grinding the heel of it as he pushed upward, and felt the nose flatten with the tearing of cartilage. Bellew released his neck, pushed him upward, and then kicked out with both feet against his chest. He came up and back, felt his head strike the mizzen boom, and sagged to his knees. Out of the corners of his eyes, he saw Rae emerging from the hatch with the shotgun barrels in her hand, raising them to swing.

Bellew whirled as lightly as a cat, caught her arm, and yanked. She came catapulting up on deck. Bellew plucked the gun barrels from her, threw them outward into the sea, and cuffed her backward across the deckhouse in three smooth and almost simultaneous blurs of motion. Ingram was on his feet again. Bellew turned back to him, grinning and hideous with blood running down his face and onto his chest from the pulpy ruin of his nose. Ingram tried to swing, and then something like the popping of a flash bulb went off inside his head and he was on the bottom of the cockpit.

He wasn't completely out, but dazed and too sick and too weak to get up. He tried. He pushed upward with his arms, felt *Saracen* roll all the way over and spin end-for-end, and collapsed again. He was under the edge of the wheel, and inches in front of his face two feet in white canvas shoes were bound to the bottom of the binnacle with a section of old heaving line. He was absorbing and cataloguing this phenomenon with the bemused wonder of a baby discovering its navel, and only beginning to fit it back into its position in a framework of time and place where everything had blown up and hadn't yet finished settling, when somewhere far off he heard the scream begin. Then the feet moved upward—quite casually, it seemed to him—and the heaving line parted as if it were rotten string.

His mind was clear now, but he still couldn't get up. He fell back on his side and was looking up past the wheel and the binnacle. Bellew, the gory face split in its wolfish grin, was leaning over Warriner. And Warriner was sitting up, cringing backward, still screaming.

"No, Daddy, Daddy, Daddy, no! No—no!"

Ingram vomited. He could feel the warmth of it on his hands, and the deck was slick with it as he tried again to push himself up. Mrs. Warriner materialized out of somewhere, flinging herself across his line of vision onto Bellew's shoulders. Bellew shrugged her off. Only half turning, he slapped her backward, and she fell on Ingram's legs.

"Come on, old Hughie-boy, old shark-killer." Bellew grabbed Warriner's shoulders and lifted. He was apparently still talking, for Ingram could see his lips move, but all sound was lost then in another cry from Warriner, a mindless, unceasing, animal screaming that lifted the hair on Ingram's scalp and ran like ice along his back. Warriner lunged upward from behind the wheel, his legs kicking free of the remaining turns of line around them. The line from his wrists to the stanchion gave way. Muscles writhed in his arms. His hands burst apart. Bellew shifted his grip, caught him about the waist, and lifted. He stepped up on the narrow strip of deck between the cockpit and the rail.

Mrs. Warriner was off Ingram's legs then, springing up and toward Bellew. Ingram made it to his knees. Warriner's cry cut off as he saw the water below him, and he spun around in Bellew's grasp, locking his arms and legs around him as if he were clinging to the bole of a tree, and nothing was visible of his eyes except the whites. Ingram got to his feet but fell backward onto the seat. *Saracen* rolled down to starboard. Bellew and Warriner began to topple outward. They were already over the lifeline and almost horizontal when Mrs. Warriner leaped out onto Bellew's back and clamped one arm around his neck while she beat at him with the other hand. All three of them, in one welded and inseparable unit, wheeled slowly over and fell into the sea.

[17]

"FLASHLIGHT!" HE SHOUTED TO RAE, WHO WAS GETTING up now. He pushed himself off the cockpit seat and raised it to grope in the locker under it for a diving mask. Leaping to the rail, he looked down. None of them had come up. Bellew, even his tremendous strength powerless in Warriner's cataleptic embrace, couldn't break free, and Mrs. Warriner wouldn't. She'd still be trying to separate them when she lost consciousness. Yanking the mask down over his face, he fell backward into the water.

He turned and peered downward but could see nothing. Farther out, the water was faintly illuminated from the spreader lights, but here directly under the side it was in deep shadow and it was impossible to see under the boat at all. He had only a minute or two at the most. *Saracen* was swinging around on the swell, and by the time he could dive twice there'd be no way of telling where they'd gone under. He kicked downward, swinging his arms in all directions, groping for them. He felt nothing.

Conscious of *Saracen*'s deadly mass plunging up and down on the swell within feet of him, he felt a moment's panic. If he lost his bearings and came up under her he could be knocked unconscious. He swam to his right and started up, and at the same instant he heard them. They were under her, bumping and kicking against the hull in their struggle. Then a beam of light penetrated the water just in front of his face. His head came out of the water. Rae was leaning over the side with a flashlight, shining it downward.

"They're underneath." He gasped. "Shine it in under the counter."

She ran back and threw herself flat on deck aft of the cockpit. Reaching an arm over, she threw the beam of light down and forward, past the rudder. He went under again. He was below the turn of the bilge now and could see the light angling down astern, but everything forward of it was in impenetrable shadow. *Saracen* plunged up and then down, rolling to starboard, toward him. He put a hand up and felt the planking, slick with marine growth, come lunging down against it. He shot downward. It stopped. Pain bit into his palm where it had been cut by a barnacle. As *Saracen* went back to port he swam down and in, raking the area with his arms. Then he saw Warriner and Bellew.

They were almost straight below him, falling away now and dropping into the beam of light. They were still locked together, but no arms or legs moved, and something like a plume of dark smoke was drifting upward and diffusing in the water above them. It was blood, either from Bellew's broken nose or from some wound inflicted on one of them by the keel or hull. He kicked downward but knew at the same time it was impossible. He was already running out of breath, and they were nearly fifteen feet below him, still drifting down. But Mrs. Warriner must be still above them. He *had* to find her. Then his hand brushed something just below him, something soft and fern-like. It was her hair. He entwined his fingers in it and began swimming up and out, away from the hull above him. His chest hurt now, and he wondered if he would make it. He'd been a fool to come under here; his first responsibility was to Rae. Just before he blacked out, his head broke surface and he gulped hungrily at the air.

He was almost under the counter, still too near the rudder and propeller. He swam out, trying to get Mrs. Warriner's head above the surface. Rae had seen him now. "Others—too far down—no use—" He gasped. "Ladder—" It would take too long to tow her around to the other side. Rae disappeared above him, and almost immediately the ladder was dropped over the starboard side, just forward of him. He swam up to it, towing the inert figure behind him. With the beating he had taken from Bellew, he was very weak now, and he wondered if he could get her aboard. Time was precious. She'd been unconscious for minutes.

He ducked under the surface and pulled her across his shoulder. When *Saracen* rolled down to starboard, he got one foot on the bottom rung of the ladder, caught a lifeline stanchion with his free hand, and heaved upward, with Rae helping from above to haul her in under the lifeline until her body was on deck. He came on up himself. They lifted her down onto one of the cockpit seats. Her hair was plastered to her face and she was bleeding from a half-dozen barnacle cuts on her bare legs and shoulders, but she appeared to be uninjured otherwise.

He turned her face downward and began applying artificial respiration. Water ran out of her mouth and drained from her hair, but there was no movement. A minute went by. Two. Three. He was on the point of turning her on her back to try the mouth-to-mouth method he'd read of when he felt her begin trying to breathe again.

She retched and began to gag from the salt water she'd swallowed. He stepped back. She was breathing regularly and without difficulty now. In a few more minutes she opened her eyes. She looked around, blankly at first, and then she screamed. She came off the seat, trying to get to her feet to lunge toward the rail where they'd all gone over. He'd been expecting it. He caught her and forced her back. She fought him, still screaming. Then just as abruptly all the strength went out of her again and she collapsed. She lay face downward while her whole body shook with sobs.

Rae had disappeared. She came running up the ladder now, carrying a glass. Between them they got her upright and forced her to drink. They eased her gently back on the cushion. In a few minutes the crying ceased and she lay still.

"What was it?" he asked.

"Codeine tablet," Rae said. She fumbled a cigarette out of her pocket, but it fell from her fingers into the bottom of the cockpit. She made as if to reach down for it, then merely sighed and collapsed on the other seat. Ingram bent and picked it up for her, but with his wet hand and the water pouring off him and down his arm it was mush by the time he'd straightened. He tossed it overboard. *Saracen* rolled. They looked at each other in silence.

Then Ingram's face twisted. "Maybe if I hadn't hit him . . ."

She looked up. Her voice was thin and very near the edge as she said, "Stop it! And never say that again. He was going to do it, no matter what you did, and you know it. And you saved her, didn't you?"

"I guess you're right."

She rubbed a hand across her face. Then she brought the hand down and looked at its trembling. She clenched it into a fist and opened it. "With luck," she said, "maybe I can keep from thinking about it for ten minutes, and keep from hearing—from hearing—" She swallowed, and went on. "That should be—just about long enough—to get her into that forward bunk and into dry pajamas and wrap a towel around her hair. And then take one of those codeine things myself. Because if I don't make it, you're going to be picking up springs and cogwheels the rest of the night. Let's go."

Ingram awoke just at dawn. He ached all over, and his stomach muscles felt as if he'd been run over by a truck. He turned his head in the beginnings of light inside the cabin and looked at Rae asleep in the opposite bunk. She was wearing the same sleeveless short pajamas she'd had on yesterday morning, and the mop of tawny hair was spread across the pillow, encircled by her arms. The only thing different was the discolored and swollen area on her face where Warriner had hit her. Just beyond his feet the tea kettle slid and bumped gently against the rails that kept it on the galley stove. Dishes shifted minutely in their stowage above the sink. A timber creaked. It was hot. And it was still dead calm.

He rolled out of the bunk and donned khaki shorts, remembering he could no longer run about the boat naked or clad only in a towel. His eyes softened as he looked down at Rae, and as he put on water for coffee he was careful to make no sound. He went up on deck. It could be yesterday morning all over again, he thought; everything topside was wet with dew, and the surface of the Pacific was as slick as oil except for the heaving of the swell. It was full daylight now, and the few clouds overhead were already edged with pink. Wind or no wind, it was morning, it was beautiful, and it was good to be alive. Then suddenly he was thinking of Warriner and Bellew somewhere in the eternal darkness and the ooze two miles below, and he swore softly as he tried to wrench his mind away. He knew that for years it would keep coming back, leaping out at him in odd moments and without warning to hit him with that unanswerable question: *Would something different, some other way, have worked?*

No. Nothing could have changed it. He'd done everything he could, and in the only way it could have been done. If he'd let Bellew's deliberate provocation go unchallenged, any control he might have had over the situation and any chance he'd have had of saving all of them would have been gone forever. Once authority was lost, you never got it back. And with Bellew doing as he pleased, Warriner would have been doomed anyway. And at some other time, particularly if they were under way, he might not have been lucky enough to save Mrs. Warriner.

He took a look around the horizon for squalls and went back below. He made the weather entries in the log and wound the chronometer. Just as he finished pouring the water through for the coffee, he heard Rae whimper in her sleep. He set the tea kettle down and stepped swiftly over beside her bunk.

Her head was turning from side to side now, and the little cry of pain or of terror was growing in her throat. He dropped to his knees and put his arms about her and began to whisper softly in her ear. She jerked spasmodically, fighting the grip of his arms, and cried out once, but then she was awake. Her eyes were wide with terror, and then confused for a moment before she relaxed and all the tension went out of her. "Just hold me for a minute," she said.

"It won't last forever. You'll quit dreaming about it."

She nodded. "I know. But it may be a long time. The rest of it you could handle, but—oh, God, if only he hadn't said that, *Daddy, Daddy, Daddy*—" Her chin began to quiver and she clenched her teeth to stop it, but tears welled up in her eyes.

"He tried to kill you," Ingram said. "Does that help any?"

"No."

"I guess it wouldn't." He was silent for a moment, and then he went on. "There's not going to be much privacy on here till we get to Papeete, so I want to tell you this now, while I can. I love you."

"That does."

"Does what?"

She managed a smile. "Helps."

He put his mouth down and whispered against her ear. "You're the only one they ever made. Nobody else could have done it—"

"Never mind the junk about what I did. Just tell me again that you love me."

He told her. Then he nodded toward the door into the forward compartment. "While I'm pouring your coffee, take a look in there and see if she's all right."

She rolled off the bunk, opened the door a crack, and peered in. She closed it and nodded. "Still sleeping quietly," she whispered.

She dressed, and they took their coffee on deck to drink it. Ingram lit a cigar, and they watched the sun come up, neither of them saying anything. She started to tremble once as she looked down at the water, but got control of it. He went below to get the compass, to see what it was going to take to secure it in the binnacle, but when he was opening the drawer he heard Mrs. Warriner moving in the forward cabin. He stepped back up the ladder and motioned to Rae. She came down. "Take her something to put on," he said quietly, "and a comb and whatever else she needs to fix herself up. I'll pour her some coffee and take it up on deck."

It was several minutes before they came up. Mrs. Warriner was wrapped in Rae's seersucker robe. Her hair was combed and there was a suggestion of lipstick on her mouth, but her eyes were dead and washed-out, and there were dark circles under them. Her movements were those of a sleep-walker as she sat down in the cockpit and accepted the cup of coffee. She said good morning and thanked him, but it was pure reflex, the ingrained and automatic good manners, and he realized she would have said the same thing if she'd been blind drunk or bleeding to death from a severed artery. But at least she hadn't come running past him to try to jump overboard again. Maybe he was going to get through to her.

She took a sip of the coffee and accepted the cigarette Rae held out to her. "Thank you," she said. She turned to Ingram. "Thank you for saving my life last night." Same tone, he thought. Same inflection. They were of equal value.

He waited till she had finished the coffee, for what strength it could give her. He was sick of making speeches and dreaded it, but it had to be done.

"You heard what he said?" he asked then, abruptly, and apparently with complete callousness. Rae looked at him wonderingly.

"Yes," Mrs. Warriner replied in the same flat tone. The pain showed in her eyes for only an instant and was replaced by that quality of deadness.

"I didn't ask because I enjoy torturing people before breakfast," Ingram went on. "I usually wait till later in the day. But what I'm driving at is that if you did hear him, you know by now it wasn't you he was slamming the door on when he slugged Bellew and left the two of you to drown. It was his father—"

"Yes. Wait," Rae broke in. "I don't know why I didn't remember it before." She told them of Warriner's strange reaction when she'd asked him if his father was still alive.

Ingram nodded. "So there you are," he went on. "He didn't blame you for anything. He didn't think you betrayed him, and he didn't think you deliberately went off and left him to drown. It's just as I told you all along; he was already irrational and didn't know what he was doing; he was confusing Bellew with his father. Probably nobody will ever know what his father did to him, but it was there in his subconscious all the time, and when his mind began to let go—" He gestured wearily. "God, I'm tired of sounding like a discount-house psychiatrist. But don't you see, that was the reason he backed down from Bellew the way he did? When Bellew started bullying him and riding him, the old patterns began to come to the surface again. But I'll get on to what I'm trying to say. You're an adult, and you've probably got more sense than I have, and if you want to go on blaming yourself for something that was never any of your fault from first to last, that's your affair. Aside from the fact that I like you and have a great deal of admiration for you, it's none of my business at all.

"But sailing this boat is my business, and there's a lot of work attached to it. You can help us, if you will, or you can make it tougher by keeping us busy heading you off from the rail because you want to go on torturing yourself like some mixed-up adolescent. Am I making any sense to you at all?"

She nodded, and for a moment there was a trace of life about her eyes, a touch of the old coolness and intelligence. "Yes, you're doing quite well." She turned to Rae. "Mrs. Ingram, I like your husband."

"I'm fond of him at times myself," Rae said.

Mrs. Warriner tossed her cigarette over the side and stood up. "What do we do first? Can I help get breakfast, or shall I be dishwasher?"

Ingram sighed gently. "The first project is that compass. As soon as I can get it installed in the binnacle some way, we'll swing ship and compensate it while we've got the sun low on the horizon. We'll need the azimuth tables, and a watch, and something to use for a new deviation card—" He broke off and stood up himself, looking out to starboard.

"What is it?" Rae asked.

"Wind."

She stood up, and they all turned to look. Off in the northeast the surface of the sea was darkening with the riffles of an advancing breeze. It might die out in ten minutes, or it might never even reach them at all, but it was wind. And today, or tomorrow, or the day after that, they'd pick up the Trades.

For further free information on new and stock titles from NO EXIT PRESS, the NO EXIT PRESS Crime Book Club and our special offers please send your name and address to:

Oldcastle Books,
18 Coleswood Rd, Harpenden, Herts, AL5 1EQ